Tales from an Irish Fireside

by

JAMES MURPHY

THE MERCIER PRESS
DUBLIN and CORK

The Mercier Press Limited
4 Bridge Street, Cork
25 Lower Abbey Street, Dublin 1

ISBN 0 85342 593 0

These stories were originally published in *Lays and Legends of Ireland* in 1912.

Printed by Litho Press Co., Midleton, Co. Cork.

CONTENTS

AT NOON BY THE RAVINE

I

'It's thinking I am there'll be bad work before long, Maury,' said Philip Farrell to his wife at the close of the May eve, as he hung up the saddle on the gowlyogue over the fireplace, having put his horse into the stable.

'Don't be talking like that, Phil,' said his wife, as she placed before him on the table a dish of white cabbage and home-made bacon, and another containing a pair of fat chickens, the pleasant odour from which would have made the most inveterate vegetarian break his resolution, at the same time turning loose out of the skeach, where they had been draining on to the table a quantity of smoking potatoes; 'it's never well to have the bad word in a body's mouth. It does not do a bit of good that ever I see. What's amiss now?'

'It's what I heard among the neighbours at the fair to-day,' said Phil, as he reached over for the tongs and drew the live turves of the fire apart to induce greater heat—at the same time heaving something that his wife's quick ear knew to be a sigh, and a heavy one.

'Botheration to it for a fair,' said Maury, heartily, 'and bad cess to the neighbours. Isn't it a pity they won't let people alone, with their stories! Not a word I'd believe that they'd say. What do they say, anyhow, Phil?'

But Phil did not reply—only looked more deeply and contemplatively into the glowing turf coals, which his wife, seeing, resolved to divert his attention from whatever painful subject occupied his thoughts.

'You're cold and tired after your journey, Phil, honey. And it's no wonder. It's sharp and raw it is, with the east wind; and its a good ten miles—no less—to the fair green of Boor-na-Bree; so it's no wonder you're cold. I'll draw the table nearer the fire, and stir it up a bit while you eat. There, sit over. That's as nice bacon as you'd get from this to the Duffrey. Maybe it's a little of something you'd like to taste before you'd take your dinner.'

But Phil shook his head and drew his chair over to the table. There was, however, none of the usual cheerfulness in his movements, and his whole air was one of subdued, if not dejected thought, seeing which his wife stirred the fire again at his side, and threw pieces of bog-wood on it, until the sparks flew in masses up the chimney, and the light reflected from the copper vessels on the dresser well nigh dimmed the gleam of the candle on the table. The sense of comfort and warmth diffused around would have made an anchorite cheerful, but it seemed to have no effect on her husband. He was silent during his dinner, and Maury wisely left him to his own thoughts undisturbed. She was curious enough to know what was the news that so distressed him; but she restrained her feelings and quietly did her best to make the surroundings still more cheerful.

'Well, well, Phil—is that all you'll eat, and you having ridden all the way this sharp evening from Boor-na-Bree! Where's your appetite gone at all?' she queried, in affectionate remonstrance, as Phil ended his dinner somewhat abruptly, and, drawing his chair towards the fire, prepared to smoke. 'What ails you at all? Is there anything amiss?'

'There's nothing amiss now; but there'll soon, I'm greatly afraid, be plenty amiss.'

'Plenty amiss!' cried Maury, in genuine alarm, seating herself by his side. 'What? What's going to be amiss? It's nothing about Aidan? No! It couldn't be!'

'No, it's nothing about Aidan,' said Phil, sinking his voice to a whisper—'The Rising. It's going to take place.'

'Yerra! you foolish man,' said Maury, much relieved, and giving him a hearty thump on the back, as she stood up from his side, 'is that the foolish talk that kept you from eating your dinner? It's the little sense you have, after all, Phil, honey, when you'd let idle talk like that bother you.'

'It's not so idle as you think,' said Phil.

'My gracious!' said his wife, unheeding his remark, 'such a thing! Why I've been hearing talk of this all the time since Christmas—Christmas! ay, and before it—and nothing has come out of it. Only that I know you, Philip Farrell, to be a sensible man, a good man, and a true man,' and Maury put her arms around her husband's neck and gave him a hug emphasising her words—'I'd think you were a fool to be listening to those foolish talkers!'

Whilst Phil smoked his pipe, in a somewhat less gloomy mood, before the roaring fire—for his wife's cheerful words had an assuring ring about them—and Maury herself felt a growing load of fear at her heart resolve itself into nothingness, and fly away, let us take our readers into our confidence and sketch the surroundings.

But, indeed, the surroundings sketch themselves, for Phil's thick white head of hair would tell at once, notwithstanding his strong, vigorous frame, that the three score and ten years of the Prophet had well-nigh passed over his head; the black hair, sonsy face, and pleased, bright expression of eye would tell you at once that his wife had not yet passed her forty-fifth year, and that in marrying at all Phil married late in life. Also the comfortable kitchen, in which, as being the warmest part of the house, Phil was now taking his dinner, together with the appliances thereof, and the long square row of out-offices, barn, cowhouses, stables, carhouses, surrounding the bawn, would show you at once that Phil belonged to the class popularly known in the country as strong farmers. If they did not, the drove of cattle returning from the fair in care of some of the farm hands, and now entering the yard under the charge of a young fellow on horseback, who, lightly leaping from his saddle, enters the house, would, beyond doubt, assure you. And when Maury says, smilingly, 'Aidan, you are welcome back. You nearly brought the nightfall with you,' it did not need Aidan's cheerful answer, 'We came as fast as we could. We're not so long behind father after all. What a grand fire you have!' to inform us that they held the position of mother and son, and that Phil when he was getting married had chosen for himself a blooming and winsome young girl, else she could at her age have scarcely been mother to this tall, broad-shouldered, strapping, beardless young fellow. Which indeed was the case.

But it did not need any dialogue at all to inform us that she was the mother to another—for that young girl entering the door just now from the dairy, with a pail in her hand, is so exact a replica of the woman inside—the same eye, the same rounded face, the same good-humoured expression, the same full lips ready on the smallest occasion to break into a smile—that there could be no mistake whatever in the matter, save and except that there was in the younger that indefinable, indescribable grace and attraction that youth lends to a pretty and sweet girl.

And passing in and leaving her pail on the ledge of the dresser, she came over to where her father was sitting, and standing behind him and placing her arms around his neck, and with her chin over his shoulder, began to whisper to him about the news of the day, until the gloom which his wife's words failed to banish completely, vanished wholly before his daughter's pleasant gossip, and gave way to a gathering-up of the wrinkles at the corner of his eyes which is usually held to indicate high good humour.

Now the nightfall having really come, and the cattle being safely housed, and the door being shut and fresh logs thrown on the fire, there was an addition to the group in the shape of another—a boy of seventeen or little over. He had been reading in the parlour during the evening, and now came to read at the lamp on the kitchen table and in the warmth of the kitchen fire. He was very different in appearance from his sister and brother; the fine flush of health that marked their faces was absent from his, and the strength and suppleness that displayed itself in their forms were lacking in his—for he was curiously slender and fragile looking, and a sense at once of timidity and delicacy was strongly apparent in face and eye—whenever he looked up from his book. Perhaps it was this gentleness and love of books that made the mother mark him out in her innermost mind for the priesthood—and caused the strongest and fondest hope of her heart to turn to the day when she should see him officiating at the altar, and when she should hear his first Mass. For to that end he was destined.

It was a very happy scene of domestic peace and comfort, this group gathered under Phil Farrell's roof-tree, as they talked over the incidents of the day—till at last they reached the subject which had troubled the good man's heart.

'Your father was saying something about the Rising, Aidan,' said his mother—'sure it isn't true?'

'Why wouldn't it be true, mother?' asked Aidan cheerily, as if it were the most agreeable subject in the world.

'Why wouldn't it be true?' echoed Maury, aghast. 'What a thing to say! I hope the people'll have more sense. What do they want?'

'What! Mother. What do people anywhere want? To be free—what else?'

'Free—are they not free enough? Haven't they plenty to eat and drink, and what more do they want?'

'Men want a great deal more than that sometimes, Irishmen as well as others,' said Aidan, a pleasant smile playing around his lips. 'If they own the land, they ought to have it —oughtn't they?'

'And sure they do—don't we own ours, only to pay rent for it. Isn't that enough?'

'Oh, I don't mean the land in that way, mother. I mean Ireland, just as the French own their land, the Prussians theirs, and so on.'

'And be killed fighting in battle, like the French and Prussians are now,' said Maury, growing a little white; for slow as communications were in these times, the news of the tremendous victories of General Buonaparte, and the miles of dead and dying strewn over his famous battlefields, was well enough known in Irish homesteads. 'God forbid anything of the kind would ever take place here. What good would it do to people when they're dead. What happens when they're gone, only to leave sore hearts and eyes red with crying after them.'

'Well, mother, people can only die once, and they must die some time,' said Aidan, agreeably. 'If people thought your way no good could ever be done anywhere. The strongest would do what he liked, and the rest would be all slaves at his bidding.'

This sort of argument by no means appealed to the mother's sense of right, and she was about to make a vigorous remonstrance against it when her husband, who had been listening in displeased silence to the discussion, said:

'There's no use talking of this any longer. There'll be fools while the world's in it. It's well for Aidan he's only a boy yet or maybe he'd be as big a fool as the rest.'

'Father,' said Aidan, gaily—his was one of the quiet natures in which pleasantness is deep-seated and hard to be ousted out of its place—'as far as that goes I'll be twenty-one come August next, and I was man enough to lead the reapers all through the ten-acre wheat-field last harvest.

'So you did, Aidan,' said his father, much pleased at the recollection; 'no better nor stronger boy of your age stands in the whole country, and travel it over from one end to the other. You'll do it again next year, please God. But—you're not a fool like other people—you wouldn't take part in their foolishness.'

'I hope I'm not,' said Aidan, with unruffled cheerfulness. 'And as to that, I hope I'll always be able to do a man's part. I'd never hold up my head in the land again if I were to be behind where others were to the fore. I'm not going to earn a name for ———'

'What's that you're saying, Aidan?' asked his mother, not quite understanding the drift of his talk, but a great lump suddenly growing at her heart. 'Sure it's not ———'

'What he's saying is idle talk and foolishness,' interrupted Mr Farrell, angrily; 'it's time for us to say the Rosary and go to bed. I'm tired after the day, and so's Aidan, too. Go on your knees.' And in obedience they all knelt, and the usual prayers were repeated.

They were just ending when the barking of the dogs outside announced that someone was coming, and presently the latch was lifted and a form entered. Evidently he was welcome, for a pleasant smile all round greeted him, and, in reply to his salutation: 'God save all here! Who comes oftener than I do?' The answer, which embodied curiously enough a deal of welcome, came:

'Those that come twice to your once, Hugh,' and all reseated themselves around the still glowing fire. If Nonnie blushed a little, nobody could notice it, for it might be merely the reflection of the firelight.

The chat was pleasant and cosy, for Hugh was looked upon, for reasons of which nobody knew better than Nonnie, as one of the family; but after a time Mr Farrell rose up and went to bed; so, too, did Kevin. Mrs Farrell, it may be remarked, was deeply religious, and had named her two boys after the patron saints respectively of Wicklow and Wexford. After some further gossip, the good woman said in a whisper:

'Hugh, isn't this queer talk that's going about?'

'What talk?'

'About the Rising.'

'Musha, God help your foolish head,' says Hugh, putting

his arm round her shoulder and giving her a hug where she sat, 'what would you be thinking of such things for? Fitter for you to go to bed and keep that ould man's back warm.'

'Hugh,' said the anxious woman, not to be put off from her intention by Hugh's deludering ways, 'Aidan I'm afraid is very foolish.'

'Is he, faith?' said Hugh. 'It's the first time ever I heard it.'

'He is, then.'

'Well, I'd rather somebody else would think that than I, when I'm making a bargain with him. He wasn't very much of a fool when he sold me that ould spavined filly for thirty pounds when it wasn't worth thirty sixpences. Ask the people at the fair of Boor-na-Bree is he a fool. It's the fright of their lives you'd give them.' Aidan's face curled into a smile and the corner of his eye puckered up with droll humour as he heard this.

''Tisn't about that I'm talking—he's clever enough that way,' said Maury; 'but I'm afraid of my life he's listening to the foolish talk of the boys.'

'Och, leave him to me. Go to bed, mother, and dream of heaven. It's the best thing you can do,' Hugh replied, with easy nonchalance.

'It's pleased I am to see him with you. There's not one in Ireland's ground I'd rather see him with, for it's yourself, Hugh, were always the sensible boy. I hope he'll take your advice and it'll do him good.' Hugh stirred uneasily but made no reply. Mrs Farrell went off to bed, and the three remaining sat chatting about anything or nothing at the fire.

At last this too ended, and Hugh rose up to go. Nonnie accompanied him to the bawn gate to fasten the hasp after him; and when Aidan, a few minutes later went on his rounds to see that all was right in the byres, he could see Hugh's figure dimly at the other side of the gate, Nonnie swinging on the lower rung at the inside, and hear her low, musical laugh as she bade her lover goodbye.

12

II

Early in the morning, shortly after dawn, Mr Farrell, as was his wont, knocked at the door of the brothers' room to waken Aidan. There was no response, and he opened the door and looked in. Looked in, only to find a sudden chill at his heart, and a sudden blindness in his eyes! For Aidan was not there. He was gone! He stepped back into the kitchen, glanced up at the rack over the fireplace—one of the two guns there was gone! Phil Farrell's heart grew colder than ever; his limbs trembled beneath him; a thick fog of darkness fell over his eyes—worse than before. He groped —literally groped—his way to the bedroom.

'Kevin! Kevin!' he cried, in awful dismay, 'can you tell me where Aidan is? Where is he gone? Do you know anything of him?'

Kevin, woken sharply out of his sleep, could tell nothing. He looked at his brother's vacant place, and said:

'I'd say he's gone over to Hugh Holmes', father; Hugh, you know, was here last night.'

Maybe he had. It was likely enough.

Phil Farrell ran out through the bawn, unfastened the gate, and went as fast as he could to the distant farmhouse. Alas! There was no good news there. Aidan was not there. Neither, for that matter, was Hugh. He too was gone. Further revelations showed that all the young men of the neighbourhood had left during the night: all were gone. There may have been more distressed men than Phil—more desolate households than his—in Wexford that fine May morning; but, if there were, there were not many. There was no need to ask where they had gone—if indeed, anyone had the courage to let their minds rest on the dreadful thought.

It is simply wonderful how fast bad news travels. It comes in the air, I do believe. Otherwise, there is a moral code of communication which the electricians have not yet found out. For Kevin, being around through the neighbouring farmhouses during the midday and afternoon, had learned that in a distant part of the county there had that very day been 'bad work'—men's lives had gone out at the point of the bayonet or pike, or the round of the bullet; and the green grass of Wexford was red with life-blood spilled. And thereafter there were white faces on the women-kind, and hearts went throbbing tumultuously under the strange weight that pressed thereon, as never they had throbbed before!

'Phil, do you know what?' said Maury, in a low voice, drying her red eyes—red with weeping—as her husband came in, wandering vacant-like from the fields in the afternoon. 'Pedher, Marshal Leger's man, was here just now looking for the loan of a plough; and do you know, I think 'twas to see if—if—everybody—was here! I'm sure 'twas never for the plough he came.'

A new light shot into old Phil's dazed eyes—but it was not a pleasant light.

'And do you know, Phil, if I were you I'd —— You know your cousins, in Thomas Street, in Dublin, have been long asking Nonnie on a visit—and if I were you I'd go with her this very night—no, not an hour would I delay—and leave her there for awhile.'

Phil looked at his wife, at her white face and her wet eyes, for some time without speaking—in that rapt mood that people have when aching thoughts are filling their brains. Then said, slowly: 'I'll go tonight, Maury; soon as the dusk falls.' And he did—he and Nonnie.

If anybody were to say there were many sleeping forms in that district that night he would not, I think, be quite correct. But if someone were to say that many fervent prayers went up to heaven from under these thatched roofs —prayers as earnest and appealing as ever arose since supplications were first made—all the long night, he, I think,

14

would be nearly right. And what a long night it was! But the nights, long or short, pass, and this one did. The morning and the forenoon also passed, and with the midday came the visitor of the previous one—Pedher, Marshal Leger's man.

'It's what the master told me to say, ma'am, that the times are growing very dangerous, and that it would be bad that a young girl like Nonnie would be here and soldiers coming. The master likes the family, and being always a good friend, and it's what he says if she were to go up to the house she'd find shelter and safety there—for he's great influence entirely with him that's over the soldiers, and she'd be safe until the troopers are gone. They're bad people, them soldiers.' Thus spoke Pedher, after some preliminary talk about the weather and the crops.

'Are the soldiers coming?' asked Mrs Farrell, with a fresh throb in her heart.

'They are, ma'am; they're not a quarter of a mile, or so much, from the head of the street now. And if I were you I'd let her come at once. I'll bring her up.'

Marshal Leger, it may be premised, was a large land owner whose house was some short distance away at the other side of the hill. He was one of the Cromwellian descendants; an inheritor of forfeited estates; a young man and a bachelor. He came of a bad breed, and he did not improve it; and was bad himself in more ways than one. He had often thrown admiring eyes on the handsome girl, and more than once Nonnie was forced to lower hers to the ground in passing him, before the bold look he bent on her. And more than once Aidan and Kevin, guessing this, had bent scowling eyes on him. But Philip Farrell, unknowing of this, or more worldly wise, always kept on good terms with him.

'The soldiers won't do us any harm no more than anyone else,' said Mrs Farrell, with a sense of deep thankfulness in her heart that her daughter was gone—which latter fact she, however, carefully kept concealed. 'Why should they?

We are all safe enough where we are.'

'I don't know about that,' said Pedher. 'It's martial law in the land now, and they may do what they like. And what they like is not the best—morebetoken, where there's —— If you'd take my advice you'd let her come.'

'I'm much obliged to Mr Leger, Pedher; and you may tell him so. He was always a good neighbour, and sure if there's any need Nonnie will go up to the house—why not? But there won't.'

'I know more than you do,' said Pedher, with a grin showing on a disappointed face. 'And, maybe if I told you you'd alter your mind. One is enough to lose in a family.'

'One! What do you mean, Pedher? What are you talking about?' asked Mrs Farrell, as the white of her eyes came where the pupils should be, while Kevin, sitting on the stairs at the window, pretending to be reading, though his eyes saw no word on the white page, looked up.

'What I say is that you'll never see Aidan again—alive, anyhow. He was hung by these same soldiers in the wood of Rahore this morning, and his body's there still, unless the rope broke. Now, don't you think ——'

Whatever query Pedher was about to put remained unspoken; for, with a wild cry, in which all a woman's fear and horror, and all a mother's love, were concentrated in passionate intensity, Mrs Farrell broke out, all her fears now culminated to a point:

'Is it Aidan? — my boy, Aidan! Hung! Hung! O, Mother of God! O! Aidan, Aidan! my son, my first born! Oh, Aidan, Aidan! — come to me! Bright love of my heart, come to me! Aidan—Aidan!' Then with her hands flung wildly above her head, and with eyes whose expression Dante has pictured when he described the awful look of those who find themselves suddenly adjudged to eternal fire, so full of morbid horror they were—she fell fainting on her back, her head only being saved from the flagged floor by the wealth of hair piled behind.

16

For a moment Kevin had jumped to his feet, too, and stood in amazed horror. He did not see, or was unable to see, his mother fall; but her despairing call echoed from his lips, and 'Aidan—Aidan!' came in a cry well nigh as replete with agony as hers! Fuller, for there was mixed with it a strain, a dreadful strain, of vengeance.

'They're coming down the street,' said Pedher, who, alarmed at the consequences of his words, had run to the door, probably with the intention of making off. 'The soldiers are coming!'

Kevin relaxed from his rigid position; and, as if actuated more by something outside him than by inward impulse, ran over to where the second gun was on the rack, took it down, gave a fleeting glance at the flint and the powder in the pan, and then, through the open doorway, flew out into the centre of the street and knelt down. The long-barrelled gun in his hand, the cap dashed back from his forehead— knelt down! Picture the scene: the long, straggling street, sloping upwards; the soft, radiant sunlight of the May day falling in a pleasant flood around; the red coats of the soldiers as they just appeared on the top of the road; and the lone figure—almost the only thing in the long, straggling street visible—kneeling there, gun in hand. Surely a strange vision of a strange time!

A flash of red light, followed by white smoke, leaps from the muzzle of the long shooting piece. There is confusion immediately in the fringe of red at the top of the street. A horse rears and plunges: evidently his master's hand grows graspless on the reins. Long-legged soldiers quickly dismount and seize the bridle. Topsy-turvy everywhere. Presently, from the confusion three soldiers speed out, and, firelocks in hand, ride swiftly down the street. Kevin Farrell's courage would seem to have been but momentary; a mere sudden impulse—arising possibly from strained excited nerves. The bullet sent speeding on its way, and, in the wreathing smoke, wholly unconscious of its

17

effect, he threw down the musket and fled.

Pedher, standing in the threshold, saw it all—thunderstruck. It was so quick, so sudden, so soon over, that he had scarcely more than time to look on. Mechanically he walked over and took up the gun the unhappy half-crazed youth had flung down. He was vaguely examining it when the rush of the troopers brought him to his senses. But the next moment the butt end of a musket descended on his forehead, staggering him to the earth. If he had intended offering explanation, it must have been offered in some other world than this; for, other infuriated soldiers riding up, a noose was quickly formed on the end of a rope, and Pedher, never more to tell a lie in this world, hung suspended from the bough of a tree!

He had told a lie at haphazard in this case, however, but it came marvellously near the truth. Along with the column of soldiers came improvised ambulance wagons—country drays requisitioned and driven by troops—and on these lay many wounded soldiers. Others—insurgents too—lay wounded and bleeding well nigh to death, and among them was Aidan Farrell!

It was well for his mother that her unconscious state prevented her seeing her gallant boy. A murderous fight, wholly unexpected, had occurred between the band of rebels marching to join the main body and the troops hurrying southwards. The former had entrenched themselves in the ruins of Kilnacree burial ground, and here, while ammunition lasted, they had kept their foes at bay, and when it was exhausted had opposed clubbed musket to bayonet point—a wholly unequal match. Aidan's beardless face was black and swollen with wounds; his eyes were closed—the discoloured eyelids drawn over them like those of the dead; and his curly hair, of which his mother was so proud, was matted with blood and dust, clogged and clotted. His coat was off—had been thrown off or torn off, and from the dusty, ragged condition of his clothes it would

18

seem as if he had been tied to the car, had been compelled to walk, had fallen from loss of blood, and had been dragged along the road, through the dust of a summer day, and had finally been pitched senseless on the top of the dray. It was one of the many hundred similar incidents which occurred then—which always occur in war times—of which the stately pages of history take no note. But, as he lay on the broad of his back, his bloody face and black eyes turned to the smiling sky, it would require keen sense to know him for the lithe, alert, active, broad-shouldered Aidan of a few days ago.

Oh! Maury Farrell, Maury Farrell! it was the good god that kept your eyes fast shut whilst this dreadful cortege rolls by.

But it did not roll by far. Below the little village street was a small piece of level ground—the village common. It was bounded on the off-side by one of these ravines so common in Ireland, of which, perhaps, the Scalp is the best sample to Dubliners, with the difference that this—the pass of Dunrahn, as it is called—seemed rather a split in the rocks, it was so narrow. The cliffs on either side went down sheerly perpendicular, and a dense mass of shrubs and underwood filled the bottom. A fairly high wall lined it at the village side, to keep children, wandering cows, and horses, and such like, from tumbling in. And here, while the afternoon was yet quite new, the column halted.

They had scarcely dismounted when Marshal Leger rode up. He was well known to the officer in command. He had heard some faint rumour at the house of what had occurred and hurried over. To his dismay he heard of Pedher's untimely end. Putting one thing with another, the colonel soon comprehended that it was not the form swinging from the bough of the tree that had shot his late trooper, and some inquiries put him on the right track. Search was made for the young culprit, who was found hiding in the hay-loft. Why he did not go further when favoured by the turmoil heaven alone knew. Perhaps some instinct of being near his mother kept him there. As he stood before the colonel and Marshal Leger it was clear enough—at least it was to those gentlemen—that whatever momentary exhibition of courage had before stirred him had now vanished. He shivered from head to foot. No aspen leaf ever quivered more than he in every nerve and muscle. Nor could he in his utter want of courage lift his eye to look at the soldier.

'Why did you fire at us?' the latter asked.

There was no response. No lip moved in speech; no eye was raised. Another would have looked with calm defiance at the questioner, and dared him. But the unhappy youth, every spark of boyish or manful fire apparently gone out of him, only shivered and shook the more.

'Why did you fire at us?'

The query was repeated in sterner tones, but it failed to elicit an answer.

'Hang him—he's only fit for a dog's death,' the colonel said in utter contempt. The noose was quickly made and flung around his neck. He did not seem to feel it. Lost to all sense of bravery, he seemed indifferent even to this. But at this juncture Marshal Leger drew the colonel aside.

'Will you do me a favour?' he said. 'They tell me this fellow's brother is a prisoner and badly wounded. You will hang or shoot him, I suppose, presently. Now, instead, offer this fellow his liberty if he shoots his brother. The fellow is craven enough to do it. He may as well do it as one of your men. It need not save his life, for you can hang him after. And no one will blame you for it, for his memory will be execrated.'

The colonel consented; he was angry at the loss of his trooper, angry at the firer of the bullet that came so close to his own life; and the whole business would be a striking lesson to the neighbourhood. With a nod to the soldiers they tightened the noose around the lad's neck until it was taut enough to give him a foretaste of what it presently would be. Then, at another, it was unwound, and the colonel said, 'See, my lad. I don't want to hang you. I'll give you your life. But it will be on one condition. See this man.' Three soldiers led forward the disabled form of his brother; supporting him, for he could not stand. His head hung limp on his breast, and it was clear enough that he had no cognisance of what was passing. The earth and the things of it were rapidly fading from his view. Kevin lifted his eyes; they fell on the helpless form of his brother, and, for the first time, a sound passed his quivering lips—a moan—a moan of abject terror—as the colonel well knew.

'See this man,' the colonel repeated, 'he is about to be shot. You can save your life by shooting him. On that condition your life is given you. Will you accept it?' There was no response from the quivering figure—perhaps in the abjectness of his terror he could not speak—but a move of the hand gave intimation sufficient of his readiness to accept the condition of saving his life.

Picture the scene once again; the level grassy common; the red-coated lines of soldiers; the limp figure tied to the pole in the centre—around which in happier days little children used to play—to keep him erect, for he could not stand himself; the forms of the old women crouching on the eminences around watching the proceedings; the colonel and Marshal Leger together on horseback; the glorious sun over all; and—the kneeling figure, musket in hand, all alone in the centre, levelling it to his eye, awaiting the word, 'Fire!'

The scene was intensely dramatic, and a shudder went unconsciously through the ranks as the colonel shouted the order. Soldiers even could not see one brother slaying another without being stirred. But a different sensation followed it, and the ranks of troopers suddenly turned stiff as stone figures, for, the kneeling stripling, swift as lightning, shifted his kneeling position, deflected his gun—and, by the ghost of King Brian!—glanced swiftly along the barrel and fired straight at the colonel; then, hidden by the wreathing smoke, ran like lightning to the wall, vaulted lightly over it, and dropped into the precipice beneath. At the same moment, the cords which held Aidan Farrell to the post gave way, or some convulsive movement burst them, and he fell prone on his face—dead.

It was this, perhaps, more than anything else that lifted the thrall of surprise in which the soldiers were held. It was not fear nor abject terror, after all, that swayed the youth! They broke through the lines, and, whilst some ran to the wall and looked downwards, musket in hand, others ran to the colonel. They were just in time to catch Marshal Leger falling from his horse. The bullet had passed through the colonel's side, opening a gaping wound—the blood was already besprinkling the saddle—but it had found a billet straight in Marshal Leger's heart.

Search was made for more than an hour in the ravine for the fugitive—so close that hardly a mouse could live there and not be discovered—but no fugitive was found. Where he could have sheltered was something more than a mystery, for the searchers entered at both ends, and escape was, humanly speaking, impossible. The eve was falling, and, with a wounded colonel, and in the face of a dangerously hostile district, it was not considered safe to keep the troops longer. They were accordingly marched off. A soldier with his foot turned over the body of Aidan Farrell—but he was dead beyond all question. A little later on in the Rebellion and his body would have been mangled with sword-cuts and bayonet-thrusts—but it takes some time, after all, before men can be turned into demons, and Aidan was spared.

The dead man was waked in the barn. I shall pass over the scenes leading up to this. But during the night one of the women-watchers though she saw something that indicated life still in the form, examined it, and found the indication to be true. Means—they were skilled in the use of herbs in those days—were promptly taken to resuscitate the body and with success. There was a funeral, however, for reasons quite obvious, but the coffin in which the corpse was brought to Dublin was pierced with holes; and weak unto the verge of death, Aidan Farrell was brought to the house which his sister had entered a few days before.

III

Troublesome times do not last always and the Rebellion and its effects passed away. Every nation whose name is recorded on the map has gone through more or less similar scenes, and, doubtless, will again, so long as hot passions stir men's hearts and warm blood pulses freely in their veins; so long, too, as resolute men spurn death where a great object is before them and strong impulses nerve them. But causes and effects pass away and it was so here. The angel of Peace once more spread his bright, composing wings over the land. An Act of Indemnity was granted; and Aidan Farrell returned home, still weak with the results of that dreadful day. So, too, came from his hiding-place Hugh Holmes, lithe of limb and pleasant of speech as ever. Fortune favours the brave, they say, and it had certainly favoured him. First and foremost wherever there was danger, reckless as if his life were of no value to him, he passed through all the perils of the time absolutely unscathed, but leaving a fame and name that still endure in the mountain valleys.

One would think that a shot was never fired in that land, that pike or bayonet was never uplifted by vengeful hands, that murderous work had never been wrought under the canopy of smoke in the streets of her towns, that evening when Nonnie Farrell and Hugh Holmes were married, or during the long night when the dance and merriment went on in the barn, and seldomer a handsomer couple stood before the priest, even in that dear land, where all the men are brave and all the girls good-looking.

But in all the revelry and merriment there was one heart —one simple, loving heart that was sad and sore—Maury Farrell's. Her thoughts were with that son—that lost son, Kevin. For curiously no word, no account, no sight, no hint had ever come from him since that memorable day when he had vaulted over the boundary wall into the ravine. He had disappeared as effectually as if the ground had opened and swallowed him. No trace, to the utter perplexity and astonishment of the people, had ever come of him.

Time rolled on—as it always does—and it brought years of peace and plenty in its train to most of our characters. Phil Farrell's white head had gone into the grave and the white daisies were growing above it. Maury's hair had whitened, too—mainly, I think, for the poor boy, whose memory was never once out of her mind. Countless were the *Paters* and *Aves*, the Rosaries, the Litanies that she offered up for her absent darling.

They had their reward, however, and Maury's eyes saw the most blessed sight they were destined to see until the golden gates of heaven opened before her, when one day the missing one returned—garbed, as her heart in the early days yearned to see him, in priestly dress, fresh from the halls of Salamanca, whither, after adventures and escapes almost beyond the pale of fiction, his wandering feet had turned.

MAUREEN'S SORROW

I

'Where did you get that ring, Maureen?'

'I was pulling up a root of the rose tree that grows in the Rath, mother. They say that a piece of the root put under your pillow will make you dream such dreams! So in tearing up the root this ring, quite bright and fresh, as you see it, turned up.'

'You shouldn't have torn up that root or disturbed the clay there, Maureen. God knows what poor fellow was laid to rest there in the old times without as much as "Lord have mercy on him", said over him. There was many a tear shed for him by those who little knew where he was laid to rest. Maureen, don't do that any more.'

'Very well, mother. I wouldn't have done it but Maury Nowlan, the cup-tosser, said the other night at the dance that any girl who put a root from that Rath under her pillow would dream of her sweetheart next night, and see him for certain. So all the girls agreed that I should do it— just for the joke, you know, mother,' said Maureen, half-repentantly, hiding her face on her mother's shoulder. 'I wouldn't do it, mother, if I thought of what you said just now, but I didn't think it was any harm; and Ulie Daly said if I saw any sweetheart it was sure to be him, and I wanted to show him to the differ. I'm sorry I pulled it up anyhow,' said Maureen; 'and if I disturbed anyone's rest why I'll pray for him tonight, and make it up with him, and you'll see we'll be friends. I'm sure there's no one in the Rath sleeping, mother, but knows I wouldn't disturb his rest. People used to call me the Fairies' Pet, you know, mother, when I was a little child.'

'And well they might, Maureen. It's well I remember the summer's day I left you sleeping in the cradle, and locked the door upon you, and went to the fields where they were making the hay. When we all wondered where the smoke was coming from, sure it's little any of us thought where it really was until we came home in the evening; and there were the four black walls of the house, and the roof that had burned away, rafters and all, smoking up from the inside where it had fallen in, and your cradle inside under it, as I thought.'

'What did you do then, mother?' asked Maureen.

'It's myself that was nearly out of my senses, and only the people held me I'd have run through the red hot fire to look for your little cradle. I was only twenty-one years of age then, and sure it's little the sense I had. Anyhow, they all gave you up for dead, and my keening and wailing might well have woke the dead in the Rath to life. The men got pitchforks to pull the burning thatch asunder, and buckets to throw water on it and quench it. If I didn't call out melia murder all the time and accuse the dead people in the Rath for not saving my child's life when there was nobody else to do it, it's no wonder. Everybody though I was mad, as I believe I was for the time. When I thought of the bright eyes of my little child, and she lying burned under the ashes, I believe I was.'

'Well, mother, and how did you find the bright-eyed little child?' asked Maureen, laughing.

'Lanna! I was crying out to the people around to give me back my child, to the saints and to the dead people, when I thought I saw a woman moving through the furze bushes in the Rath. I could only see her red cloak. But I grasped at the thought that maybe she might have saved my child; and I tore myself away and ran to the spot where I had seen her, and then I found yourself lying asleep under a bush just as I

26

had left you in the cradle.'

'Did you see the old woman, mother, and what did she say?'

'I didn't remember anything more, for I fainted, until I awoke in a neighbour's house, where they carried me, to find you safe and sound. But the men searched every place, high and low, through all the bushes in the Rath, and there was no sign of a woman to be seen. It wouldn't be easy for them to see her.

'It was the Good People that saved my darling's life, and ever after they called her the Fairies' Pet. That's the reason you ought to think kindly, Maureen, of the people that are lying there. You remember long ago how you used to pray for them—that the sun might shine brightly on them.'

'But, mother,' said Maureen gaily, 'maybe I really was burned, and it was only somebody else's little child you found, thinking it was your own. Anyhow, mother, I pray for them still; and don't I always take care to plant flowers in the Rath, and are not the rose trees that make it so beautiful planted by my hands? Have I not always kept the cows from trampling there, and is there any place on the farm kept so well? Mother, sure it would be no harm in the world if I did what the old fortune-teller said. It wouldn't do them a bit of harm, and I shouldn't love them a bit the less.'

'Maureen,' said her father, who laid down the Irish Prayerbook he had been reading during this gossip, 'don't do anything of the kind. Not to speak of its being vain and sinful to try and see what's in the future, and unbecoming for a girl to speak of such subjects, it is wrong to use the dust of the dead for any such purpose. Let them sleep in quiet peacefulness, and don't disturb them even in thought. I have lived here nearly fifty years, and I feel proud that during that time I have not done anything to disturb their resting place. It is pleasant to feel that when I go out in the morning and come back in the evening I have not done any-

27

thing to disturb their repose. We have lived and prospered beside them; they were good friends to us in many a way; and we were lucky in everything we took in hands. I always feel when I am away, and always did when your mother was but a girl, I might say, and you a baby, that they were keeping kindly watch over you in my absence, and that you were safe in their keeping.'

'Very well, father; but didn't we always take care of them. Don't we leave the fire burning brightly every winter night for them to come in and sit at if they are cold and weary? Don't we leave the cream-crocks uncovered for them to drink at, if they will? But anyway I wonder who owned this ring or what brought it here?'

Maureen tried the gold wedding ring on her finger and found it a little too large.

II

It will be clear from this dialogue that Onie Donovan was a simple, kind-hearted man, and that his wife was equally so. Owen—Onie they called him for shortness sake—was a thriving farmer, and he lived where the townland of Bahana sloped to the south, the sun and the woods of the Roer. At one side, deep down below its wooded banks, ran the goodly stream of the gladsome Barrow; in its front deep in the valley, too, was the abbey which Moling—saint and seer —erected thirteen hundred years ago; to its left lay the long range of the beautiful Blackstairs, and at the other side across the river lay Ballyogan with Brandon Hill towering at its back. The saint when he was building his abbey had an eye for the beauties of nature, for no more picturesque or romantic a place could be found in all Ireland. Fronting the farmyard was a large green field, and one corner of this adjoining the house was covered with furze bushes, whin bushes, and rose trees, which latter Maureen's hand had trained to grow there. This was the Rath. Here the bones of men, long forgotten, were laid to rest. How they came there no one knew. It might have been the burial place of some old sept, of which no memory remained. They might have fallen in battle for the freedom of their native hills and glens—as men have in Ireland before, and probably may again. Or it might have been the burying ground of those in our pagan forefathers' times before the light of Christian faith was borne to us across the seas by Patrick. There were the graves, at any rate, and they were carefully tended by these good and simple people.

It will be clear, moreover, that Maureen was somewhat of a spoiled child; and if gentle and kindly in her nature, was also slightly wilful and capricious. But what will not be quite so apparent to my readers, until I tell them, was that the fairest rose that was planted by Maureen's white hand could not in its brightest glow have equalled her own simple and graceful loveliness. Her eyes seemed to have borrowed their brightness from the summer rays that slanted to her mother's door over the Blackstairs, or even at evening, across the slopes of Brandon Hill; and surely the deepest recess in the woods of Bahana was not so dark and deep as they in their unfathomable beauty.

It was but little wonder, then, that the sleeping tenants of the Rath—if all that is kindly and pure and affectionate in our nature does not die out (as I have firm faith it does not) with our lives—should take her under their special care and loving watchfulness. Maureen had pledged herself to her mother not to put her girlish whim into practice; but Maureen was a pure daughter of Mother Eve, and she longed to taste of the forbidden knowledge of futurity, promised by the old fortune-teller. So next day, when there was no one by, she took with her a knife and cut another root of the rose tree that was growing on the unknown grave, and carefully concealed it in her bosom.

'They won't mind me,' thought Maureen, smiling to her-

29

self, 'doing it, for I'm their Pet; and I'll plant another rose tree and the fairest flowers of spring over their graves in return.'

Poor Maureen! She felt unhappy and uncomfortable enough, nevertheless, during the evening; and to escape any discourse similar to that of the preceding night, or any return to the topic that was likely to elicit the truth, for she would have scorned to equivocate about it, if questioned on the subject—she retired to bed earlier than usual.

III

Whether Maureen dreamed the dream she had expected, or whether, if she did, it did not in its anticipated fulfilment bring that pleasure she had counted on; or whether she had looked into the future and seen her coaxing sweetheart, she never divulged. But certain it is that her face was paler and her manner more serious and solemn that was her wont when she came to the breakfast table next morning, and her eyes looked as if she had, from some cause or another, been weeping.

The next evening the little family group was, as usual, around the fire. It was some time after dusk, and they were reciting the Rosary in Irish by the light of the blazing fire, and the strips of bogwood, known as skithogs, before retiring for the night. The father was reading it aloud, the wife and daugher making the responses—when suddenly he stopped.

'Did you speak?' inquired he of his wife.

'No,' said she, somewhat surprised at the question. 'I said nothing except the prayers.'

'Did you not say, "Lost, lost, lost"?' he asked again, with a curious expression in his eyes.

'No,' said his wife.

'Did you, Maureen?'

'No,' said Maureen, 'I said nothing but the prayers.'

Mr Donovan paused for a moment, and then continued the prayer. He stopped again, while a shudder ran through his wife and daughter.

'Who spoke? — who said "Lost, lost, lost"?'

'No one,' replied both wife and daughter.

'You did, Maureen. If ever you spoke, it was you said it.'

'I did not, father dear,' said Maureen. 'I said nothing.'

'Then pray to God to guard us, for there is something strange about me.'

'The blessing of God be around us,' came with a shudder from the lips of mother and daughter; whilst in the silence that ensued there did seem to be a sort of intangible and half-whispered conversation through the room.

Maureen, with a shiver, nestled closer to her mother. In the action of doing so she paused, for, outside the door in the bawn, a voice cried:

'Lost, lost! Open the door! A light. For God's sake, a light. Lost—lost—lost!'

Onie Donovan jumped to his feet and ran to the door. To unfasten the bolt and raise the latch was the work of an instant; and when the door opened four men appeared bearing the barn door, which had been taken off its hinges for the purpose, between them. On the door was stretched what seemed to be a human form with a white sheet thrown over it. The bearers moved past him without saying a word and placed their burden on the floor. At this moment an in-gush of night air through the open door extinguished the lights, and left the room, with the exception of the fire-light, in complete darkness.

Very much to their surprise, when they were again able to re-light, they found that the bearers had taken their departure, silently and unceremoniously. There was no one present but the muffled form that lay still on the floor—more terrible hidden behind its shrouding than it could possibly be if exposed to view.

'God bless us all! Where are they gone to?' exclaimed Onie, in dismay, when he saw they were gone. But Maureen was too much frightened to reply. Shading the torch-light with his hand, he stepped outside into the night; but there was nothing to be seen. He called aloud. 'Anyone there? Come back!—for God's sake come back!' But no reply arose on the night air.

He closed the door, having waited awhile for a response, but had scarcely done so, when a voice called aloud—it might have been at the back of the house, it might have been down the chimney—for the voice seemed to come from anywhere and everywhere—

'Open the door! A light, a light! Lost! lost! lost!'

Onie, though being what the neighbours called a quiet, easy-going man, had a great deal of natural courage lying latent in him, so, though much surprised at the sudden disappearance of the strange men, he was but little daunted by it, and concluded from appearances that they had good reasons for their hurried departure.

When he returned, therefore, he gave his attention to the wounded form that lay on the floor. He uncovered the white shrouding that hid it, and there was disclosed to his eyes the face of a young man, apparently in a death-trance. His features were pale and emotionless, his eyes glazed and sightless. There was, too, a curious expression of pain in his compressed lips, as if he were dying in great agony. His beard, which was long and silken, fell over his breast, and the ends were saturated with blood that welled up from a wound in his chest beneath.

The sight of the dying man banished the nervous fear that held possession of the women, and roused into activity all the kindly sympathies of their nature. Mrs Donovan, who was skilled in herbs, and, indeed, was generally doctress to all the poor for miles around, opened the dying man's coat, and found a punctured wound over his heart, through which the life current was welling rapidly forth. His dress

32

was of the richest description, and of very antique fashion, and he wore in his belt, which was drawn close round him and fastened with a clasp of gold in the centre, a hatchet or battle-axe, curiously wrought, and a skeane, gold-hilted of glittering brightness.

IV

The eyes of Maureen glanced rapidly from the dying man to a picture over the chimney piece which she had found long ago in the Rath, and which had hung there unnoticed ever since. The dress of the man in the picture was exactly similar to that of the stranger. There was the belt and gold clasp, the flowing beard, and the hatchet and skeane. She had no time to mention the circumstance, for her father was busily engaged placing a feather pillow under the stranger's head, while her mother was preparing some herbs, of which she always had a store at hand for staunching the wound. This she skilfully succeeded in doing, and his pain seemed in a great degree alleviated, judging from the appearance of his face.

Still the man moved not his eyes, or manifested tokens of consciousness. With the exception of the more peaceable expression on his face and the cessation of the flow of blood there was no further change in him. It had now passed midnight, and Onie, thinking there was but little chance of the patient recovering, said:

'I think I ought to go for the priest.'

'Do, Onie,' said the wife, 'he'll hardly be alive when you come back. There's hardly a stir in his pulse at all.'

She held up the hand that lay beside him so feebly. A fine muscular hand, with a red mark on one finger, as if a ring but lately removed had left its trace there.

'He must have been robbed,' said Onie, noticing this. 'Has his money been taken from him?'

'I don't know. I don't like to try till the priest comes,' said his wife. 'Oh, Onie, make haste and bring him. It's a poor thing to let him die without the blessing of the priest, anyway.'

'Will you be afraid while I'm away—you and Maureen?'

'Oh, what matter about our fear—it can't be helped. Maureen, dear, get your father some money; he'll want it to bring some spirits for the poor man.'

Maureen took down from a nook in the wall behind some hanks of flax, a twisted purse, made from the foot of an old stocking, which she untied with some difficulty, and then, dipping her hand into it, took from the bottom a gold guinea piece which she handed her father. Re-tying the purse, she replaced it in its position.

Onie went on his way full of alarms for the safety of his wife and daughter; but full also of anxiety lest the unfortunate youth should not live to receive the last rites of the church. Maureen and her mother sat in the dim firelight watching the dying man. They conversed some time in subdued whispers until a heavy drowsiness came over them.

'A light there! Open the door! A light! Lost—lost—lost!'

These words were again cried aloud; it might have been within the room, so clear and distinct did they fall on their ears, startling them from their slumbers. They both, in great terror, fell on their knees, repeating the Litany; and Maureen cried out that strange people were passing between her and the firelight.

The gray mists were beginning to pass from the sides of the Blackstairs, and the first rays of the dawn to appear on the Brandon Hill, when Onie lifted the latch of his door. The priest had not been at home, and he was obliged to return without him. His step on the floor woke his wife, who had fallen asleep where she knelt. The skithogs had burned out, and the turf fire was covered and hidden with grey ashes—the waning ashes, popularly then known as the 'Greeshuck'.

yet alight. He looked upon Maureen's face where she lay in bed—sleeping soundly. Not knowing what to think, he called in her ear, 'Maureen!'

Maureen awoke with that appearance of surprise and sleepiness which people generally have when suddenly awakened. There was clearly no pretence on her part—she had been sound asleep.

'Oh, father is that you?' said Maureen with a faint smile. 'What brought you out of your bed this hour of the night?'

'I came to see if you wanted anything, darling—if you wanted a drink,' said Onie, as the most reasonable answer that suggested itself to him. 'Have you been sleeping, Maureen?'

'Yes, father; sleeping soundly. Why do you ask?'

'Because I was afraid you were not. I thought you might be looking at the moonlight, darling.'

'No, father; I slept soundly since you went to bed.'

Onie sat by his daughter's bedside until morning. He had sufficient faith in her word to know that she spoke the truth; but—how then account for her presence in the Rath? Had his eyes, worn with restlessness and grief, and want of sleep, deceived him, and conjured up her appearance where she was not? It was hopeless to tell. So Onie sat by her bedside until the moonlight gave place to the coming dawn.

Onie told the story to his wife, who was as much perplexed as himself. The resolved that one or other should sit up with her in her room every night. A few nights after this her mother was sitting up with her. Onie awoke from his sleep and an irresistible desire possessed him to go to the window.

The moonlight was not quite so clear as before; but, in the indistinct light, he saw clearly enough Maureen retracing her steps from the Rath. She walked slowly, her eyes still on the ground, as if searching for something. She passed again in through the up-raised window, and he could hear her distinctly let down the window when she entered. He hurried down, but the candle was burning on the table as before; his wife was sitting, her head resting on the table, fast asleep; and Maureen again in bed, sleeping soundly. His presence in the room woke his wife at once. Bending to whisper to her, he asked her if she had heard anything. She said she had not.

'Maureen was again in the Rath—she only came back just now through the window,' said the distracted father, wringing his hands.

'That's impossible,' said his wife. 'She could not stir without my hearing her.'

'I saw her. I saw her as plainly as I see you now,' said Onie. 'She's only just come in.'

The noise of the whispering woke Maureen from her sleep. From a sound sleep, too, as the mother beckoned Onie, with her eyes, to see in proof of her not having stirred.

If the poor people were in grief and doubt before, their fret and dismay now were something dismal to behold. Their belief was that their daughter was bewitched; for whilst Onie could not but credit the sight of his eyes, when he saw her in the moonlight, the soundness of the sleep in which she seemed to be wrapped a minute afterwards was unmistakable.

VI

Matters were at this pitch when one day an old woman—a stranger—came into the house looking for alms. She was an old grey-haired woman; and had but one arm. She sat in the corner by the fireside, and on enquiring after the family's health, as was usual, the poor mother related the story of her daughter's illness to her.

The old woman listened keenly to the tale; to Maureen's finding the ring, to the appearance of the dying man, as well as to the apparition her husband had seen.

'What did you do with the ring?' the old woman asked when she had finished. 'Maybe she hadn't a right to touch that.'

'I don't know what Maureen did with it,' said the mother. 'I never thought about it since she fell sick.'

'It's my belief,' said the old woman, 'that Maureen will never get well until that ring is left where it was found. It's never right to take what belongs to the dead—God rest them!'

Having received the alms and a drink of fresh milk she took her departure.

The mother seized on the idea at once. But there was no ring to be found. Maureen could give no account of it. She had not seen it since that night when the dying man was brought in. She had lost it that night off her finger. A search was made for the ring, high and low, everywhere, but no trace of it could be found. There was not a portion of the floor that was not swept and brushed again and again, every nook and cranny, every hole and corner was made the centre of searchers, but to no purpose. There was no ring to be found. No, not anywhere.

About a week after this the old woman again made her appearance. Maureen was apparently in a dying state. Her mother was crooning in a seat by the bedside, swaying herself to and fro in an agony of grief and desolation. The old woman resumed her old seat.

'How is Maureen?' she asked.

'Oh, very bad—very bad entirely,' said the heart-broken mother. 'She's dying now.'

'Did you get the ring, that you told me about?'

'We searched for it everywhere and couldn't find it.' The mother wrung her hands as she made answer.

'Well, it can't be helped. Troubles will come to us all. I have a grandson myself dying, and I could cure him if I had two or three guineas to buy what I want. Two or three guineas would save my darling's life. But it can't be helped

—it can't be helped.'

'If that would save his life,' said the weeping mother, kindly, 'sure I'll give them to you, and welcome. I know what trouble is too well myself not to try to keep it from another.'

So saying she went for the purse, and opening it she gave the old woman three guinea pieces. As she started putting the rest back she uttered a scream and fell on her knees.

'The ring!—the ring! Oh, thanks be to God!—here's the ring.'

The ring was, indeed, there—having been dropped in it by Maureen when she was giving the guinea to her father.

'Give me the ring,' said the old woman, eagerly. 'And here are some herbs that I brought with me. Make a drink of them for Maureen and maybe they'd do her good. That the blessing of the charitable may be around you and yours!'

The old woman seized the ring eagerly, placed it in her breast, drew the hood of her grey cloak over her head, and went her way.

The mother did as she was asked, and gave the drink to her daughter; and Maureen slept the sleep of death for forty-eight hours after. But she awoke from her trance, and when she did she awoke in health. Her eye had its old brightness; her laugh its old gaiety; her manner its old cheerfulness. She soon recovered her former bounding health, and the roses by degrees came back to her cheek; and Maureen was herself again. Not very long after she married Ulic Daly.

For years and years they lived in happiness and prosperity beside the Rath; and children, sons and daughters, grew around her hearth in beauty and promise. And now comes the strangest part of my story.

The country had passed from a balm into a period—it was coming to the year '98—of the greatest trouble. Armies were marching over the land; and the young men and old of the Blackstairs Mountains were up in arms and arrayed against them. The green banner of Ireland was again floating; and they who had heart and spirit and strength were summoned to guard it. From Scollogh Gap to Killam, and around to St Mullins, the hardy sons of Carlow and of Wexford arrayed themselves beneath it. Among others that went were Maureen's two sons.

One June night when the family were on their knees saying the Rosary as they were wont to do in the times of old, and they were offering a concluding prayer for the safety of the two boys that were away, a voice cried aloud in the bawn, exactly as it had twenty-five years before:

'Lost, lost! Open the door! A light, for God's sake, a light! Lost! lost! lost!'

Ulic rushed to the door, opened it, and the old scene was repeated.

Four men bore the bleeding form of her eldest son on the barn door into the room and laid him on the floor. There was a white sheet over him; but it needed not to be uncovered to tell the mother who lay beneath. And exactly as had been done five and twenty years before, the four men in the darkness and confusion took their departure to provide for their own safety.

The youth had been killed that day at the Battle of Ross, where the cause was lost, and the heart of the nation lay broken and bleeding!

They had borne him home faithfully. And, like to the former occurrence, he bore hatchet and skeane in his belt; and they showed signs of having done good service on that unfortunate day. From glen and valley in the fair Counties of Carlow and Wexford—from Borris-Idrone to Sheilmalure—there went up at intervals, all through that summer night, the despairing cry of 'Lost! lost!'

There may be people who may disbelieve this story; but there are stranger things in heaven and on earth than are dreamt of in philosophy.

THE MIDNIGHT TRAIN

It was in the dreary Christmas time. The weather had been rough and bad, and a smart fall of snow heralded the approaching festival. With it had come, not the bright sparkling weather that usually accompanies snow at this particular season, but a dull, gloomy, oppressive atmosphere which made the surroundings very miserable.

Very miserable indeed. The fogs—arising maybe from the half melted snow, perhaps from the vapour-laden condition of the air—hung about all day, but grew greater as the night fell. They hung around the fields, over the embankments, and completely shut out from view the mountain range in the distance. Somehow they seemed to me to gather most thickly of all by the old ruined mansion that stood beside the deep, newly-made cutting of the railway—from which, indeed, it was only separated by the embankment and the wire fencing that ran along it.

It might have been merely imagination on my part—I was always given to fanciful imaginings—due to the dismantled condition of the ruin—which was enough to give even the sunlight of a summer day a cheerless expression—but it might also have been the actual case; for the deep cutting in the railway was a likely enough place to give birth to fogs and vapours, sufficient to fill the air around and rend it heavier and denser in the immediate neighbourhood of the old castle of Barrymore. Whether this was really so or not I could not exactly say; but it certainly did seem to me, as I came along with my gun in hand and my bag strapped lightly across my back—it is some years now since I have been home for the Christmas holidays—that that particular place looked much darker than its surroundings; and, when proceeding along the path that led along the embankment to it, I came closer, I fancied rightly or wrongly that there was some curious change in the atmosphere I breathed.

The day had been gloomy and dark, and the eve was beginning to fall. Curious to see whether the change was merely my imagination or reality, I stopped to look at the ruin. The path by which I was making my way led, as I have said, between Barrymore Castle and the railway embankment; and as I looked up the sashless windows and ivy-clad walls were wreathed around with a thick grey fog, which appeared to grow outward from the walls as if it had its origin inside.

A good deal higher up the ivy hung loose or had separated from the wall, blown about by a storm; but looking, as seen through the enveloping haze, most curiously like the form of a man suspended from the height. The resemblance was so startling that for a moment I paused to look more steadily at it with a feeling which, if not fear, was certainly not pleasure. The more I gazed at it, too, the more curiously like was the apparition. I could note the suspended form, the head, the feet, the drooping face, the fallen arms, the —

'You're too early! It's not due yet,' said a voice close at hand, sending an electric thrill through me that made me almost leap from the ground. I looked hastily around. Then all at once I saw—and wondered I had not seen before—a man standing in the broken doorway of the castle, leaning with his shoulder against the jamb. My sudden start and surprise vanished in the moment. The incident was a natural one enough.

'You're too early; it's not due yet,' he repeated, coming out a little into the fog and abandoning his leaning position.

'What's not due yet?' I asked rather sharply, for the sudden start had put me about.

'No, it's not due yet,' he said again, evidently not heeding my question. 'I knew you were listening for it.'

'Listening for what?' I queried afresh with some curiosity, for the man's appearance occupied my thoughts at the moment. 'What was I listening for?'

'The train,' he said.

'What train?' I asked.

'The midnight train,' he replied.

'There is no such train,' I informed him, quietly, for I knew.

'Oh, yes, there is,' he said quickly.

'I fancy you are mistaken,' I said. 'There is no train now until tomorrow morning. The last train for today passed an hour ago.'

'No,' he said. 'The train runs at midnight now. But you can hear it long before it comes. Ever so long. I thought you were listening for it just now.'

'You must be mistaken,' I said, wondering what on earth put that idea into his head. 'No trains run this line after the afternoon train—not until next morning.'

'It passes through the cutting every night for the past week, one minute before the midnight hours strikes. I wonder what it runs for! I thought you were listening for it, because you can hear it rumbling—rumbling—hours before it comes. At least I can.'

He spoke earnestly and impressively, and I looked at him sharply and inquisitively. I knew very well that what he was saying was untrue; no train ran at that hour; yet he certainly seemed from his manner of speaking to believe it himself.

Now, the place where I chanced to be staying for my Christmas holidays was a friend's house not more than a mile from ruined Barrymore Castle, and I was at present after a hard day's shooting retracing my steps homewards. The house stood also beside the railway; and as, in consequence, perhaps, of my visit, we were rather late stayers-up, the midnight hour was not infrequently long passed before conversation around the fire ceased and the household retired. It was so the previous night, for I remember seeing the clock at the head of the stairs as I went to bed, and the hour was near one. No train, therefore, could have passed without our hearing it, even if there had been one on the company's timetable, which there was not I knew well. Had a chance special been run we should not alone have heard it, but the very fact of such an unusual occurrence taking place would at once have attracted attention and made it the subject of remark. These thoughts ran through my mind as I looked at him.

Looking at him, in the grey gloom of the fog and the falling evening, he appeared to be a man past fifty years though still in the full vigour of life. His face, as far as I could make out, was massive and firm, with that peculiar tuft of hair on his chin which sojourners in America so much affect. This confirmed me in an impression which from a peculiar intonation in his voice I had instantaneously formed when he first spoke — he had been abroad, in America. His manner was sensible and collected, notwithstanding what he said, and there was no lurking attempt, I felt sure, to chaff or 'barrack' me. His whole demeanour and appearance forbade even the very idea of this. He was perfectly sincere.

'I am certain you must be mistaken,' I said, after a pause. 'No train ran at midnight last night, or I should have heard it. I live near the ——'

'It ran last night—it runs every night,' he repeated with decision, interrupting me, but with a strain of wonderment or perplexity in his voice that attracted my attention. 'I wonder what it is for. It is not on their timetable—midnight.'

'You are quite right there. Certainly it is not,' I said, ready to agree with him on this point if I could on no other. 'I know the running of the trains well.'

'That's what surprises me,' he said, in puzzled wonderment. 'What do they run it for? I am scarcely asleep when it thunders by and wakes me up! I jump up, and run to the window to see—but it is passed! What is it so constantly running for at that hour?'

'Are you quite sure you hear it?' I asked. 'Could it not be possible that you merely dreamt it?'

He looked at me vaguely. I think that the unhesitating certainty that he was mistaken, which was in my mind, must have expressed itself in my words. For—he turned angrily around—he was glancing down the line by which the train should come—as if he momentarily expected it, and said:

'What! Hear it? Of course I hear it. It wakes me out of my sleep! Hear it! To be sure I do. I hear it all the evening after dusk sets in. Hear it coming—dozens, scores of miles away.'

'Do you hear it now?' I asked, incredulously.

He walked a step or two backwards to where he had been leaning when he accosted me, and resumed his old position—placing his ear to the wall to listen. I knew now what he had been doing when I disturbed him, and when he so suddenly accosted me.

'Yes. I hear it plainly. It's actually flying forward. Listen, and hear it yourself!'

Curious to find out how it was he was so illusioned, and whether some rumbling noises might not be in the air, I took up the position he had vacated; and, placing my ear to the wall as he had done, listened. Nor sound nor echo was there—not, at any rate, that I could hear, and my hearing was acute. If he had really heard anything it was a something that was not palpable to my ear. And I said so.

For reply he brushed past me angrily and entered the ruined abode. I was surprised. For a moment I stood surprised. My first feeling was one of regret that I should have contradicted him so openly when there was no necessity for so doing; my next was that the sooner I got away from the place the better. I don't know why this latter sensation

pipe. 'We are in no hurry. Go on with your story. I am sure it will be interesting.'

'It would be interesting enough if I could tell it properly,' said my host, stirring the fire into a blaze. 'You never heard of Hardress Rutherford?'

'No,' said I, 'I hadn't the pleasure. Who was he?'

'No, of course you didn't. How foolish of me to ask!'

'Well, never mind! What of him?'

'This: Hardress Rutherford lived in that house. So, for that matter, did his father before him, and his father before him, and so on. They came over with Oliver Cromwell, I believe. At any rate they owned some generations ago—they got it during the confiscations—all the land for miles around. They were a bad lot. But what with extravagances of one kind or another—but always of an evil kind and in an evil direction—they sold or mortgaged the greater portion of the property.

'It may have been their own fault, it may have been the workings of fate—"Ill got ill gone", you know—but anyhow part with it they did, until, in Hardress Rutherford's time it had been reduced to the townland surrounding the Castle and the Castle itself. Even then Barrymore looked splendid and imposing, and showed but little sign of their diminished fortunes; and as for Hardress himself, he held his head as high as when they could not see the extent of their estates from the highest windows of the mansion. It was hard for these Saxon invaders to see themselves coming down in the world—albeit they paid mighty little for the land originally. They stepped into the shoes of the old Catholic lords, who were forced into exile and driven to join the Continental armies.'

'It was during his time Barrymore then got ruined?' I asked—anxious to get to the kernel of his story.

'Don't be in a hurry,' said he. 'Let me tell it my own way. Yes, it was in his time it became ruined.'

'How did it occur?'

'You are very impatient. Well, it was this way: You see, Hardress Rutherford was a widower, with an only son, Oswald Rutherford. Whatever evil habits belonged to the family in past times—and they were numerous—it was certain that few of them were inherited by Oswald. Perhaps that was because he had an Irish Catholic mother. A handsomer, gayer, pleasanter young fellow could not be found in the whole country around. From his earliest days he mixed with the people as if he were one of themselves. And as the years went on, he grew in the estimation of his neighbours, until they began to regard him as warmly as if he could trace his descent from the oldest stock in the land, instead of from the Cromwellian freebooter of two centuries before. In the hunting field amongst the gentry, there was none so manly, so handsome, or so bold and skilful a rider as he; and when he mixed with the people and took part in their footballing or hurling, or other athletic sports he bore the palm from all competitors. There was not the slightest bit of stuck-up-ness about him. He was as pleasant and free and agreeable among our young folk as if he were one of themselves—one of their own kith and kin—never making the slightest difference with them.'

There was a pause here, and my host seemed sunk in reflection over these vanished times. To break his reveries and get him on with the story, I said: 'Oswald Rutherford must have been an exceptional young fellow?'

'You may well say that,' he continued. 'There was not one in the whole country more beloved by the people. They would have died for him, notwithstanding the bad and evil race he came from. And when it became known that he was about to marry Miss Everard—'

'Who?' I asked, not catching the name clearly.

'Miss Grace Everard, daughter of Colonel Everard, of Beaumont Hall.'

'Well? Go on.'

'Miss Grace Everard was just as beautiful a girl, at the

time, as you would see of a summer's day. Wealthy, too. And everyone—everyone of the people, at any rate—was glad of Oswald's good luck. It was not to be wondered at, however, for it you were to see them in the hunting field together, he with his handsome figure and sitting in the saddle as if the horse and he were one, and she with her sweet face and drooping eyes—which shone brighter than the sunlight, when she looked up—you would see at once they were made for one another. And everyone said what a plucky, high-spirited girl she was to throw aside all considerations of rank and wealth, and give her hand and estates and love to the handsome but penniless young fellow. His good luck and high prospects made no change in him whatever. He was just the same as before—affable, pleasant, friendly, and mingling with the people on equal terms. There was not one, I think, even among the gentry, that grudged him his bright fortunes.

'Yes, there was one; I except one—Hector Malverston, of Bentogher. And he was anxious—and well he might—to secure her for himself. He was rich, and he was very well connected—he was cousin to the Marquis of Beadalmore; but his rank and wealth could not win favour in her eyes when Oswald Rutherford was to the fore. Grace Everard preferred her handsome lover, with his open heart, manly figure, and winning address to all the broad estates in Westmeath. And everybody praised her for it.'

'Well, how did it all end?' I asked.

'You shall hear. A handsome and wealthy heiress was not to be let slip away so readily as that—nor a penniless half-sir, as Malverston called him, to bear her away without challenge or interruption.

'The projected wedding gave rise to much animosity and ill-will on the part of Hector Malverston—and to ill-will, open or secret, between the two, one result of which was that they quarrelled at last at the Grand Hunt Ball at Athlone. Oswald Rutherford, for some insulting words said, struck his rival with his horsewhip on the doorsteps of the County Club, and gave him a tremendous horsewhipping before they could be separated. Fortunately, or unfortunately—which way you like to look at it—Grace Everard was not present that night at the ball, and did not therefore witness this quarrel, of which, no doubt, she was the cause and centre—though I believe Rutherford always affirmed that her name had nothing whatever to do with it.'

'And had it not?'

'Well, of course, nobody could very well tell. Rutherford said it had not; but most people had their own opinion on the subject.   We all guessed pretty well what was at the foot of it.   There was to be a duel, of course.'

'Well, how did that come?'

'It never came off.'

'No! Why?'

'Before the day appointed Oswald Rutherford was behind the iron bars and stone walls of a prison, out of which as a free man he was never more to go.'

'Eh! What! Not for that surely!' I exclaimed.

'No—not for that.'

'What, then?'

'Murder.'

'Murder! Good heavens! — No!'

'Murder. For murder, wilful and red-handed! Murder, such as cries to the listening skies for vengeance—and is seldom unanswered!'

'Gracious heavens! That is an awful story!' I could not help exclaiming; and, in my exceeding surprise, letting the pipe fall and breaking it. 'What had he done? Killed Malverston?'

'No. That would not have been so bad. But, on the way as you go from this to Bentogher, nearly midway, indeed, between the two places, Barrymore and Bentogher, there lived hard by the Shannon banks, a farmer, Forrestal by name. He had children, many children; but the eldest was a girl—and such a girl! I remember her as well as if it were yesterday. It would be hard to forget her face once you saw it. One might as well try to forget in a dungeon the sight of the sun, or the sea, or the bright face of the earth on a summer's morning. She was the rarest girl for beauty that ever graced a farmer's homestead. Brighter eyes than hers never looked on the flowing Shannon since first its waters gushed forth and flowed. It was a rare gift—that gift of beauty—seldom given, not once in generations; but it was a fatal gift to her, poor girl! Her exceeding good looks attracted many visitors, eager to see one so richly endowed.

'Among others that called there, many times passing by, was Oswald Rutherford. We have a saying down here, when we want to describe one of a bad race, "The black drop is in him." It was true enough it turned out of this fellow too. The blood of the Cromwellian trooper, the merciless raider, and the burner, was in his veins, disguise it with smooth manner and speech as he might—was in him to the back-bone! The body of the wronged girl, slain by his hand, was found in the valley, almost in sight of her father's house, hard by the banks of the smiling Shannon!'

'The Lord bless us and save us! — No!' I exclaimed, horrified at this unexpected denouement. 'No! It could not be. There was some mistake!'

'No mistake whatever,' said my host. 'It could be—and was. Why he did not fling the body into the rushing stream, no one could tell. Perhaps he was unable; perhaps horror unnerved him; perhaps he fled fearing detection. Whether that was so or not, at any rate to the affright and horror of all the people the body was found as I have said; and Oswald Rutherford was arrested, lodged in jail, and placed on his trial for murder—and found guilty!'

'Oh no,' I said. 'Don't say that.'

I could say no more. It was with difficulty I could say so much, for all my senses revolted against this denouement. It came on me like a nightmare of horror after what he had previously said. If he were one of these idle villains who follow the worthless craft of novel-writing he could not have led up to it more skilfully. But he did not intend that at all.

'Yes, found guilty; and most justly so,' said he, firmly. 'For, strangely enough, of all men to see him leave the place, not knowing what frightful deed his hand had done, was his rival—Hector Malverston.'

'But surely,' I said, 'no one would take his word or listen to his evidence after what had happened?'

'His huntsman was riding behind him; and he, too, saw Rutherford slink away from the place. Others, too, saw him going along the public road near the place late that night. But the fragment of paper—the torn remnant of the marriage certificate—in her clenched dead hand explained all. They had been secretly married, it would appear. But it was the one insurmountable barrier to his marriage with Miss Grace Everard; and to possess himself of it he did not hesitate to rend the life of the sweetest and fairest rose that ever bloomed by the Shannon banks—many a one as grew there!'

'Gracious skies!' I said. 'I am sorry you told me this sorrowful story. I shall not feel the better of it tonight. He was hanged, I suppose?'

'He was found guilty and sentenced to be hanged. The evidence against him was too convincing now—Mr Malverston and his huntsman having seen him leave that particular place just about that particular time; others having seen him on the road near; his constantly calling to her house when passing to and fro—though indeed that was not an unusual thing with others—and—and——'

'The name on the marriage certificate,' I suggested, interrupting him a little.

'Well, no. Curiously, there was no name on the fragment she held clutched in her hand—the important portion had been torn off. But there was no need. Everyone knew what fatal and unlucky name was on the missing part. It needed no sworn evidence. It was a visible to the jurors' eyes as if it were there in black and white during the days of his trial and on the darkening eve when the judge sentenced him to be hanged!'

'And he was hanged?' I asked. I was going to add 'poor fellow' for the narrator in the previous portion of the story had impressed me so favourably with regard to him that not even the latter portion of the terrible tale could wholly do away with the impression. So much power is there in first impressions that I almost felt as sorry for, as horrified at, the murderer. But I fortunately caught myself in time, or I should have shocked my host considerably.

'No,' he replied.

'No!'

'No. By one of these strange events that sometimes occur, he broke from his prison bonds—these places were not as carefully guarded then as they are now—before his sentence could be executed, and escaped. He was, as I told you, a fellow of fearless courage and iron nerve (or, heaven knows, he would never have lifted his hand with murderous intent against his gentle and beautiful victim), and iron bars and prison walls were but small things to him when he made up his mind to escape. They might as well have been brown paper.'

'That is a very singular story,' I said, throwing some pieces of wood on the fire to make it blaze up, for an eerie feeling was around me, and there was a most uncomfortable tingling down my back. The fire, before this, had waned and grown dark; the window at my back, looking out on the railway, was unshuttered, and the night was looking in at us grimly. 'What became of him, finally?'

'Nobody knows. The only thing certain about him is that the night of his escape he made his way to Beaumont Hall. He had the daring and audacity to visit Grace Everard there; but whatever he had to say to her must have remained unsaid and unheard, for the poor young lady was found in a dead swoon when the servants entered the drawing-room next morning. Frightened at sight of him, I suppose. He must have also intended murdering Mr Hector Malverston; for that gentleman, looking out from his window during the summer night, saw him scaling the garden wall outside his bedroom. However, he fired a revolver at him, and Rutherford disappeared. That was the last heard of him. He was never again seen by mortal eyes.'

'No?'

'No, never. But the oddest thing in connection with the matter is that his father, Hardress Rutherford, was found dead in his bed next morning. He had sold or mortgaged all his remaining property to provide for his son's defence. The amount received must have been fairly considerable, much more than was needed—only a minor portion of it could have been spent. Yet there was none of it to be found in the apartment where he died—nor anywhere in the mansion.'

'What was supposed to have become of it?'

'It is not difficult to guess what became of it,' said my host, rising from his seat and taking the bedroom candle in his hand. 'What became of it but that his scoundrel son must have entered the house during the night and taken it. He frightened, at the same time, the old man into a fit which ended in his death.'

'I am sorry I asked you to tell the story,' I remarked, as we said "goodnight" at my bedroom door, 'it has left a most uncomfortable impression on my mind.'

'There are strange stories,' he said, 'in every family. More perhaps in the old houses of Westmeath than elsewhere. Goodnight; pleasant dreams. Do not let your mind dwell on this.'

I retired to rest, but not to sleep. I could not help thinking of the story I had heard, and of the convict's escape. Also, I could not help thinking of the ruined mansion of Barrymore; the strange character I had met at the doorway;

and the curious hallucination that possessed him about the midnight train. Was he mad? Had he been drinking? He did not look like it; but either was the only possible explanation of the matter. I was very tired, and what with the thinking and the tiredness after a long time fell asleep, and began dreaming.

Naturally, my thoughts reverted to the subject of our late conversation, and, in imagination, I stood once again with the strange man at the ruined mansion. I saw him place his ear to the wall to listen, and I did the same. To my exceeding astonishment and alarm, I could hear the rumble of an approaching train! — could hear it growing in volume of sound as it came nearer and nearer. In vague terror, I listened, spell-bound, until unable to hear it longer, I started away from the place.

In the action I awoke! The noise that was in my dreaming brain was in my awakened ear, but much louder and more palpable! There was the rush and roar of a train, clear enough on the silent night!

I leaped up and ran to the window. I has scarcely reached it when, out under the arches of the bridge, some distance away, two red eyes suddenly flashed, and the house shook and the windows rattled, as, in the black gloom, a blacker object shot past, with a whirl and roar.

I stood listening for some time, until its echoes died away in the distance. There was not, after all, much to be surprised at in the passing of a train; it might have been a special put on for some urgency; but, nevertheless, I stood breathless at the window until its retreating rumble ceased.

Then I was angry with myself for my unaccountable fears. And yet—I could not get rid of them! Sleep, for the present, was out of the question, so I bolted the shutters, lit a candle, and, taking a book, commenced to read. My thoughts, however, were but little on my book, for, presently, there grew up in my mind a curious idea. I don't know what put it into my head—but come it did.

It was this—'What if that strange man, standing by that ruined doorway, had been killed by that train!'

I had often read and heard of people having presentiments of their own deaths, by violence, long before they occurred; and I began to think that the train just passed, though not at the hour mentioned, might have been the one he heard in imagination, and that by some unfortunate mischance it might have been the bearer of sudden death to him.

Stranger things had happened in men's experiences! And this man was not at all unlikely, judging from his curious talk and manner, to put himself in the way of an accident. In fact, by degrees, the words of my book failed altogether to catch my eyes, and I could only think of—and see in imagination—a mangled and shattered form lying on the rails in front of ruined Barrymore!

The sensation grew more vivid and tormenting each half-hour that passed, until, unable any longer to restrain myself, I leaped up and opened the window. The room seemed to be suffocating, and I needed fresh air. With the opened shutters came in a burst of grey light, and then I saw the dawn had come.

Far in the distance, to my right, the mountain tops were tinged with a faint reddish hue, and it was easy enough to see in an indistinct way the railway tracks in front of me. My mind was made up in a moment. I slipped down the stairs quietly, opened the halldoor, closed it gently after me, and took my way along the line. I almost shuddered to think of what I might see on the railway track at the end of my walk.

The dawn at this time of year, though slow in coming, when it does come, breaks quickly, and it so happened, therefore, that though I walked with rapid steps, it was clear daylight when I reached my destination. I climbed over the embankment when I came near the place, descended to the line, and walked along to where the deep cutting

'Was the spirit of vengeance ever shown among the people?' I asked.

'Oh, yes, frequently,' he replied. 'How could you expect otherwise? He had more escapes—more narrow shaves—than would terrify any ordinary man.'

'Indeed!'

'Yes.'

'How was that? I am curious to hear.'

'I see you are,' he said, smiling. 'Well, for one case: On this very road, where we are driving now, and not very far from this spot, a brace of pistols were fired point blank in broad daylight at him, and so close that the blaze scorched his riding coat—yet he got off scatheless. The hands that fired were nerved by hate and vengeance too strongly, one would think, to let him escape—and yet he did.'

'And they?'

'Well, they got off too. There was no one every punished for it, at any rate. But that is not all—nor the least. He has had his horse shot under him; he has seen the flash of musket across the hedge, as he rode homewards at dusk, half-a-score times if he has seen it once, and yet he has passed unharmed! What do you think of that?'

'Well, I must say he has better luck than honester men,' I replied.

'I don't know that either,' he replied thoughtfully. 'He may be reserved for worse things. It is a very awful thing for a man to have the deadly hate and vengeance of an oppressed people for ever confronting him. The history of every nation in the world is full of awful doings arising from that same cause.'

I agreed cordially. I had been reading some time before about the Sicilian Vespers, and other things of the kind, so I knew very well what reward tyranny and oppression have met in other lands besides Ireland.

'He may change from that,' I said, 'if he is so capricious he may at any moment change his hand.'

'Not in the right way,' he said decisively. 'No, not in the right way. In fact, he is more determined than ever to carry out his evil caprices. Look at that mission we are bent on now. Look at that case of poor Simon Forristal. One would think that his troubles alone would have caused him to be spared further worry. But, no!'

'What objection has he taken to him?'

'No one knows.'

'Does he want the land himself?'

'Not at all. It is not bordering on or near his demesne.'

'Forristal is a decent man?'

'The best. A good farmer, a good neighbour, and hard-working.'

'What reason can he have for these harsh proceedings so?'

'The Lord only knows.'

'Is there any use in going to intercede with a man like that?' I asked again.

'I don't know. I could not say. He is so very capricious you never could tell.'

'Ah!'

'Yes.'

'He may listen to me, and he may not. He may agree to what I say; or, on the other hand, it is quite possible the very fact of my interceding for them may so harden him that no power on earth could stay his arm. It is perfectly impossible to guess beforehand what he may do.'

'It is an unpleasant country and a dangerous business,' I said, after a pause; for it struck me strongly there would be an ugly ending to these proceedings sooner or later.

'Well, we can only hope for the best. God is good, and He may soften his heart. The great apostle was a persecutor of the Christians in his time, you know.'

I did not myself think there was much comparison between the apostle St Paul and a Westmeath evicting land-lord, but I said nothing. I was cautious to see this formid-able personage. I could, indeed, vaguely remember having read in our English newspapers some account of such outrages, but failed to connect them with any particular name or locality. However, as we drove along they grew out more strongly in my memory.

A large castellated building, embosomed in woods, was before us. To this we were bound. Bentogher , in fact. Approaching it we had to drive across a rustic bridge that spanned a small stream. Turning around a corner our horse swerved a little as a figure, dressed in grey tweed, carrying a gun on his shoulder and leading a large dog on a leash, stepped aside out of the way.

'Mr Malverston!' my friend exclaimed in hurried salutation. Then reined up. I had now time to look at this gentleman, for my companion, having exchanged a cordial greeting with him, descended from the trap to speak to him. I was very much puzzled. He certainly seemed to be very different from what I had expected. Quiet, composed, and by no means ill-looking—in fact very much the contrary—he was the very last in the world with whose appearance I would associate the stories I had been told, or the acts of tyranny related. There was assuredly in his mild and pleasant face no sign of the malignant cruelty and heartlessness of which I had heard.

His hair and flowing beard were growing grey—much too soon for his seeming age; but this only tended to give him a more agreeable and cheerful presence. Of all men he was the one apparently to whom might be entrusted that absolute power over his fellow-men which an Irish landlord then possessed. I augured a favourable reception for my companion's entreaties from the agreeable manner in which he received them—I was not near enough to hear what they said—and from the bland and acquiescing smiles with which he punctuated my friend's earnest and pressing talk. After some time another gentleman in a smart stylish trap drove up from the direction we had come, stopped and jumped lightly down when he came to them. Mr Malverston had evidently been waiting for him. They shook hands immediately. With a friendly and most affable smile Mr Malverston then dismissed my companion, who at once came over to me; climbed up into his place in the trap beside me, took the reins, and we drove off.

'Well,' I remarked, satisfied from their parting that the result had been satisfactory, 'you did a good morning's work for the poor Forristal family at any rate?'

'I am not quite so certain of that,' he answered dubiously. 'No?'

'No.'

'I am very sorry to hear it.'

'No. I am very much afraid it may turn out the other way. He simply said he would think it over, and when he says that I infer the worst. From that—and his pleasant manner.'

'His pleasant manner?'

'Yes. That, most of all. When he seems in that gracious friendly mood the devil is not far from his elbow.'

I felt uncomfortable. I was very much disappointed indeed, for I thought up to this he had been successful. As we drove homewards he told me of some further peculiarities of Mr Malverston; and they led me to think he was correct in auguring ill. It appeared then that the gentleman in question was never in so bland a humour as when about to do a cruelly harsh thing; never so kind and affable as when projecting something merciless. There seemed to exist in his nature an innate tendency to evil that made him actually exult at the thought of the suffering and hardship it lay in his power to inflict, a regular attribute of the devil; as I at the moment thought, and said so!

Very shortly afterwards he drove past at very rapid speed, hurrying to the railway station with his gentleman visitor—who I afterwards learned was the police officer of the district. They seemed to be both bound for the railway station to catch the up-train to Dublin—just then due. It was with a feeling of annoyance I could not exactly account for, seeing that I had no direct or personal interest in the matter, that after returning home I once again shouldered my gun and set off to the moors.

It was not a very successful nor a very pleasant day's shooting. All day the thoughts of the unhappy man over whose head the sword of eviction was hanging, was in my brain; as also was the sad story of his beautiful but unhappy daughter; and, mingling curiously with them, was my friend of the ruined castle of Barrymore. It was no wonder my day's shooting went a bit astray.

Talking of my friend at Barrymore, I felt very curious to learn if he were there still. And if he were, whether he was possessed by the same curious idea. Wherefore it was, that, though I was full of a nervous, uncomfortable impression, I determined to pass that way again on my way home. Which I did. The fog was clinging to the ruin, as before; and the dusk was falling as I came near. I could not see him around or about as I approached, but passing by the doorway I looked keenly, and beheld to my intense surprise he was there! Still there. Notwithstanding the fact of my looking out for him and expecting him, I was still greatly astonished to see him there. I started somewhat.

'You're too early again,' he said, leaving the doorway and advancing a few steps, addressing me. 'It won't be here for hours yet.'

'What won't be here?'

I asked the question in embarrassment. I knew well what he meant, but in the momentary start I could form no other rejoinder.

'The train,' he answered, sharply. 'It won't be here for hours yet. Not until midnight.'

'It did not run last night at midnight,' I said hesitatingly.

'Yes,' he said. 'It did. It ran last night. Eleven fifty-nine. Just one minute before the clock struck twelve it swept past. I wonder what it ran for? Do you know? Does anyone about here know?'

I knew this was not the case. So I thought it better to dispel, if I could, this curious illusion, and said stoutly: 'I was awake until after twelve. I live beside the railway. I was looking out on the track immediately before and after that hour, and no train passed. It could not without my seeing it.'

'You are mistaken,' he said, irritably. 'It did pass. At eleven fifty-nine to the minute. Full of armed men! What could it mean? Have you heard of anything happening down the line?'

'A train passed towards morning,' I suggested; 'perhaps that is the one you heard?'

'No. I heard no train, or saw none, but the one. One minute to midnight. At that hour—always at that hour—it runs! I wonder why! What can it be for?'

A thought was growing in my mind, as he stood with hands clasped, looking in deep thought and perplexity on to the track. For there was a far-away look of troubled fear —perhaps it was scarcely fear—and pain in his face and eyes, as he gazed vacantly before him, relaxing for the moment into unconsciousness of my presence.

'Can you still hear it coming?' I asked, after a pause.

'Eh! What?'

He started violently out of his reverie.

'Can you still hear the train coming?'

'Coming! Yes. But it's very far off. Miles—scores of miles!'

I was very puzzled.

'Do you sleep here?' I asked, nodding to the ruin.

It was rather an abrupt question to ask, and I only asked because he said he did not hear the express flying by at the dawn.

The question affronted him, though, dear knows, I did not mean it to be offensive in the slightest; and, turning quickly on his heel, he walked back through the ruined doorway. Even as he did I could see that, from some strange attraction or perhaps from frequent habit, he bent towards the wall to hear again the imaginary rumbling noise! So full was his mind of it that even thus hurrying past, he could not avoid listening for it!

I walked slowly homeward; our interview thus abruptly concluded. The curious idea referred to that had grown into my head developed itself as I went on. It was a curious thing to lay hold of my mind, but it did, and grew stronger and stronger as I proceeded homewards. It was this:

This was the man of whom my friend had spoken—Oswald Rutherford. He had come back, outcast and demented, to the home of his father. Who else could it be? Come back, in all probability, spurred by an all-powerful fate to the scenes of his dreadful deed. Spurred on, also, by the singular impulse that prompts a murderer to visit the spot where he had broken into the awful House of Life, and so to bring himself within the hands of justice! Such things had happened before—hundreds of times—and something of the same kind was about to happen now again, I made no doubt. I was greatly disquieted and uncomfortable, and was by no means pleased that I should have become an unwitting acquaintance of his. And then I made the resolve that I should put myself in his way no more; I made a firm resolution to this effect.

When I reached home I was naturally very anxious to meet my host alone and talk with him over the matter. I could not get a private chat with him until dinner was over, and after; but, when the night had waned somewhat, I invited him up to my room to have a chat. After we had kindled up, and otherwise refreshed ourselves, I told him of the incidents which had occurred to me in connection with ruined Barrymore and of the suspicions I entertained. But he only laughed heartily at them.

'I am afraid you have been finding a mare's nest,' he said gaily. 'It is only some one playing a trick upon you. You are known here—a Cockney from London, perfectly innocent of Ireland and the Irish—and they would not ask better fun —the country fellows around—than frightening you. City people are looked upon as so timid. Cockney folk especially so. I wonder they did not try a better plan, though.'

'I hardly think it is that,' I said. 'It does not look like it. There was very little attempt at joking.'

'You never could tell what these fellows are up to,' said my host. 'And they think getting hold of a Cockney is rare value. They think he is so easily frightened in a strange place.' I did not altogether agree with this explanation, nor, indeed, did I like it. However, his statement, though by no means flattering to my courage personally, which I flattered myself was not small, was somewhat reassuring. He knew the ways of his neighbours best. So, as I was unwilling to dwell longer on the matter, we talked of other things until the logs on the hearth began to burn out and wane, and the cold air of the outside to make itself felt in the room.

'I rather fancy,' he said at last, knocking the ashes out of his pipe, 'it is time to retire. I did not intend stopping up so late, for I intended calling upon Mr Malverston again in the morning; but your conversation kept me and — good heavens! what is that?'

The house shook palpably; the windows rattled, and a dull, booming sound came heavily through the fog! The dull boom, before we had time to speak or make any remark, quickened and deepened into a roar, and immediately the house shook with the whirl of a train flying thundering past. We had scarcely time to reach the window when the two red head-lights, like eyes glaring through the fog and staring up at us, flew screaming by. With a violent shriek, too, which struck me in my sudden start as almost menacing and human.

'11.59,' said my friend, after a breathless pause, glancing at the clock on the mantelpiece. 'By Jove! that's very strange. Good Heavens!'

It was strange—passing strange! So strange, indeed, that we resumed our seats involuntarily, to recollect ourselves and talk it over. We were both, as may be expected, a little startled. I repeated the incident of my strange acquaintance, and laid stress on the certainty—the perplexing certainty—with which the man seemed to hear the rumbling sound of the coming train. We talked over it so long that, unable to make further explanation of it, we both relapsed into silence. The silence was, however, soon broken by a hurried rapping at the hall door—the knocks quickly becoming louder and louder.

'What is that? Who is that? Who on earth can be coming at this hour of the night?' exclaimed my host, arising suddenly from his seat. 'I hope there is nothing on fire—it could not be that the folk downstairs did not put out their fires before going to bed.'

And thereupon he left the room.

He did not, however, go downstairs; he went into another room, whose window overlooked the hall-door—on the steps leading to which the party knocking must have been standing. I could hear him, leaning out through the open window, speak to someone below. I could only hear the tones; I could not tell what he said; and I could only hear the half-audible replies of the person below in reply. Presently he shut down the window with a bang, and came hurriedly back into my room.

'Put on your overcoat—quick—and come with me,' he said.

He was very pale and greatly agitated.

'What's amiss? Is there anything wrong? Where are you going?' I asked in return, noticing his startled and hurried demeanour. 'What's amiss?'

'That train has met with an accident. There is not a moment to be lost. Come along.'

This for startling answer.

He raced down the stairs, threw open the hall-door, and

rushed out. Jumping to my feet, I rushed down the stairs after him across the lawn, over the stile, and on to the foot-track that led beside the permanent way. The night was fairly bright; he was running as fast as he could; and I was running after, keeping up with difficulty. I think the distance to the ruined castle of Barrymore—it was not more than a mile — was never traversed in shorter space. Yet it seemed an awful length of time before we came to it. But when we did, what a sight there was to behold! — What an awful sight! An accident had indeed happened. That was perfectly clear. A terrible accident!

The locomotive was lying against the wall of the deep cutting, on its side; its fires still burning or scattered about. The carriages, heaped on one another in woeful confusion, were shattered and twisted and broken—mere matchwood and bent iron! Light were moving about among the debris; and, as we came nearer, we could see that men were bearing burdens—how well we knew what burdens these were! — up the steep sides of the embankment into the ruined mansion. And, as we came still nearer, we could see to our astonishment that the bearers were all in uniform—were, in fact, soldiers. Soldiers—the lights falling on their disclosed uniform. What had brought them there?

'What had brought them there?' 'And what had happened to the train?' These were the questions that at once presented themselves to our minds. But there was no time for asking them or making any inquiries, for many mangled forms were still locked up and held down among the tangled, smashed debris; some silent, some moaning aloud; so we applied ourselves at once to the task of relief. There was no time to do anything but help and relieve as best we could the injured and suffering who were caught and held firmly by the timbers of the broken carriages in all manner of agonised positions. These, as far as we could, we helped to free and bear up to a shelter—from which many of them were destined never to be removed alive—in ruined Barrymore, which, with its sightless eyes of windows, looked down upon us.

How long we worked I do not know. We took no note of time. The occasion was not one for it. We assisted as best we could and strenuously; until once I was startled as we laid down our dreadful burden by my companion's hand, laid with nervous and quick touch on my shoulder, calling my attention evidently to something.

Gracious heavens! Oh my! look there!'

I looked in the direction—in the direction where his out-stretched hand pointed. And, looking, I saw, stretched at full length, lying on a sort of ambulance roughly made from the broken timbers of the train, the man whom I had seen full of life and strength in the morning—Hector Malverston! Yes; no other. There was no mistaking his appearance. I had seen him only on the one occasion, but his face had remain-ed firmly fixed on my mind. He lay quite rigid and motion-less; but his eyes were watchful and intelligent, gleaming bright and attentive from out of the extraordinary pallor of his face. Save, at times, a curiously surprised or frightened expression in them, there was nothing to indicate that he had been hurt. Yet, I knew that he had. The perfectly still, stirless form, with an old rug thrown over it, told eloquent-ly of the crushed mangled limbs beneath. But even yet the determination of a strong, if cruel and remorseless heart, in presence of heavy agony, gleamed from his eyes. I could see that. I had scarcely time to note so much, however—and to note it with great shock—when, lifting my eyes, I was sur-prised—yes, amid all the torture and death around, surprised —to see the tall form of the strange man, handcuffed, and in the custody of two or three constables.

He looked, in passing, steadily down at the injured form, under the coverlet beneath him; and, following the direction of his glance, I saw that it was bent on Mr Malverston's face. Its intensity was fully returned by the latter. The anxiety and astonishment of his glance, as he returned the rapt look with interest, was something that can never leave my mind! It was a strange weird scene; but it was impossible to remain watching it longer when so much necessary imperative work remained to be done. So I hurried down again to the cutting where the wrecked train with its load of misery was. When I returned with my sad load to the apartment my companion was arising from his kneeling position by the side of Mr Malverston, where he had apparently been listening to some communication the injured man had whispered to him.

He saw me, and, quickly coming to me, said:

'I am going to Athlone. I shall be back in an hour or two. Attend to Mr Malverston, and see that he gets whatever he needs until the doctors arrive. I shall go and return as quickly as I possibly can.'

I scarcely remember how that time passed. The groans of the wounded—the dark shadows stealing over the faces of the dying—the calls and cries of workers outside—the gleaming lights here and there and everywhere—made such a scene as seldom man's eyes have looked upon save in the hospitals after the carnage of a great battle is over. Bye and bye the medical men began to arrive. And whilst yet I was wondering what my friend had so hurriedly departed for, he came driving up to the place—the horse which carried him almost spent. Another gentleman accompanied him.

Mr Malverston had been meantime carried to a room where he was alone. His position and standing, even amid the havoc around, suggested a separate apartment, and ruined and roofless though it was, the consideration showed how, even amid the horrors of sudden death, worldly concerns still have weight. Into this were promptly ushered the two men—my friend merely whispering to me, as he passed, that his companion was a well-known Athlone solicitor.

'Keep watch here,' he said, 'and let no one enter.'

The faint grey light of the Christmas morning was arising dimly around, finding its way through the cracks and crevices of building, before he again came out and beckoned me inside. When I did there were but three living men there —the doctor, the solicitor, and my friend. The glazed eyes of the wounded man were fast sinking back in the chilling grasp of death, and his spirit had just passed to that mysterious land where there are no evictions—where landlord and tenant are equal.

'This is a strange business,' my friend said to me.

'What?' I asked, not knowing to what he alluded.

'Hector Malverston is dead. He has made a revelation to the attorney here. Do you know what? The murderer of Alice Forristal was not Oswald Rutherford, but himself. So he confessed. He could not—he dared not—bring the shocking crime on his soul, unconfessed into the next world. Heaven forgive him; he is in God's hands now.'

My friend blessed himself, as he thought of the dread Judgment Seat, and I did likewise.

'And Oswald!' I asked in a breathless whisper.

'Is that man whom you saw handcuffed just now. The solicitor, who is also a magistrate, will have him released presently. The confession he holds in his hands explains all.'

The gentleman to whom he referred held in his hands a few pages of foolscap on which the ink was not yet dry.

'What brought him here?' I asked, nodding towards the now inanimate form.

'He was bringing down a company of soldiers for the eviction tomorrow, and for the arrest of the stranger, of whose return he had in some way got inkling. He was bringing them in a special train hired for the occasion, and there, you see, is the end of it!'

Oswald Rutherford was promptly released, by order of the magistrate, and he assisted—so I have heard—in doing all he could for the sufferers. But when morning came he was nowhere to be seen, nor ever after. Where he had gone to, how he had so suddenly disappeared, no one could tell. No one had seen him go.

'Was it not strange—passing strange,' my friend said some days after, as we parted at the railway station, I on my return home, 'how could he have imagined that midnight train? It had not been ordered until the midday of that day. No one could previously have known of it. No one could, seeing that it had not been previously thought of.'

'It is—very strange,' I answered. 'It almost passes belief. But he was quite positive about it. He seemed to hear it constantly—it was always in his ears.'

'Do you think—do you think—it was a real living man you were speaking to?'

'Real living man! Why, what else could he ——'

'I don't know,' said my friend dubiously, 'but it is something more than singular how he could have known days before about that midnight train, and almost as singular how he could have disappeared without anyone seeing him —as if he had gone down into the earth or up into the clouds. Depend upon it, there is something in it beyond what you or I know.'

Some years after I was in Paris, and the memories of that time had nearly died out of my head, or were only remembered at long intervals and on odd occasions. Walking down the Rue de Rivoli one morning my attention was attracted by a very beautiful lady coming towards me, accompanied by a gentleman.

My eye was irresistibly attracted by her sweet and gentle face. As she passed me I glanced at her companion. My heart stood still as I did so, for in the grave and courtly lineaments of his face I recognised the man who stood in the fog in the doorway of the ruined mansion. They passed me, and were lost in the crowd.

When I returned to London my wife said to me: 'I had a letter from Limerick yesterday. Do you know who has got married?'

'No.'

'Miss Grace Everard, of Beaumont Hall.'

'What—no!' I said, remembering my late vision.

'Yes, indeed; so father writes.'

'To whom? And where?'

'To an American gentleman. No one knows his name.'

HANDWRITING ON THE WALL

I

'There's someone knocking at the hall-door, sir.'

'A sick call, I suppose.'

'I dare say it is, sir. The knocking has been going on for some time.'

'You had better see who it is.'

'Shall I admit him, sir?'

'First ascertain his business. Then come and tell me. I hope it is not a sick call.'

The priest said this wearily. He was sitting at the parlour fire reading his Office, with his boots off. He had just returned from a sick call in a distant part of his mountainy parish, and was now taking a rest. His spattered apparel showed the narrow and slushed lanes through which his route had lain, and the fatigue of the day was evidenced in his jaded face.

As soon as the old housekeeper left the room he laid his Breviary aside and stirred the blazing wood which burned in the grate, sending up the chimney a myriad of sparks. He passed his hand through his hair, which was white as snow, as he said again, with a patient, wearied expression: 'I hope it is not a sick call—I hope, indeed, it is not a sick call.'

'Who is it, Mary?' said he, as the housekeeper re-entered the room.

'A man, sir, that says he wants to see you.'

'Is it a sick call?'

'No, sir, I don't think it is. He says he wants to see you on business.'

'Very well, Mary,' he said, glad that he was not compelled again to face the night, for he was very tired. 'I'll let him in myself, though,' he said, as he stood up. 'It's a curious hour for any person to come on business—why, it's nearly eleven o'clock,' glancing at his watch.

The priest passed out to the hall-door and opened it. The night was somewhat dark, and the light of the lamp was in his eyes, so that it was some time before he could make out objects outside. However, when his eyes became sufficiently accustomed to the darkness there grew into distinctness before him, standing a foot or so from the steps, the figure of a man.

'You want to see me?' said the priest.

'I do, your reverence. I want to speak to you, if you please. Only for a minute or so.'

He appeared to be bareheaded, but as he spoke he carried his hand respectfully to his forehead in salute, and then the priest noticed that he carried his cap in his hand. His voice was the voice of one in deep mental distress. The priest, holding the door open, said, 'Come in.' He passed into the hall crouching-like, and the priest, closing the door, led the way into the parlour. He resumed his seat at the fire, and the stranger sat somewhat to his right, a little in the shade. The priest sat a little while waiting for the man to speak, but he did not. He appeared to be at a loss how to commence.

'You wanted to speak to me, I think,' said he encouragingly.

'Your reverence,' said the man, fumbling with his cap, 'I did want to speak to you. I often wanted to speak to you, and I put it off from time to time. But I can't bear it any longer.'

'Bear what?' said the priest, gently. 'You haven't told me what?'

'That's what I can't well tell you,' said the man with an effort, 'It's what's over me—there's something over me.'

77

'Something over you!' returned the priest. 'What is it— what's the nature of it? Are you ill?'

The kindly manner in which he spoke, and probably his venerable appearance, encouraged the man to unbosom himself of what, it was evident, was a painful subject to him. He moved closer to the fire, with a shivering motion as if he was cold, and as he came within reach of the fire the priest noticed that his face was thin and worn, as if he had been suffering from severe illness.

'I haven't been well, indeed, your reverence,' he said, still fumbling with his cap, 'but it is not of that I have to complain. I'd have been well enough in my health only for that.'

'Only for that?'

'Only for that,' returned the man. 'It's two years since— ay, since I saw it first. I was sitting in my cabin. I live, your reverence, in Glenruven, up among the mountains.'

'Yes, yes,' said the priest, 'I have heard something about that. Your name is Moghan, is it not?'

'It is, your reverence—that's my name for certain,' said the man.

'Well, let me hear it now. I called sometimes, but could not get in. There was nobody in your house.'

'Likely enough there wasn't, your reverence. I'm mostly out looking after the sheep—through the mountains. I don't care to be much in, particularly in the daylight. It comes mostly in the daylight.'

The priest looked at him sharply. He had heard some curious things about this man, though he had never seen him before, and what he had heard led him to regard him with great interest.

'What is it?' he inquired, with quiet gentleness, 'that comes chiefly in daylight?'

'It. What I'm speaking of. I first saw it two years ago. 'Twas one day in the summer time. I was all the morning through the mountains of Dunmore, and through Glen-

78

scalthagh—the sheep had gone astray—maybe the dogs had sent them astray—maybe someone was trying to steal them. How do I know? Anyhow I was weary and tired before I got them together again. I came home and lay down on some heath beside the fire to sleep. 'Twas about twelve o'clock before I got home. I lay down, as I said, to rest myself, and I slept a long time, for I was tired. I might have slept three or four hours. I don't know what time it was when I awoke. I got up and shook myself thoroughly awake. The sheep will be in the White Lands over Balvorna by this time, at any rate, says I, looking round for my staff. I couldn't find it by my side where I put it, and I searched round the room for it, when all of a sudden I saw something stretched on a table. It was It.'

'It?'

'It. The form of a dead man. God between us and all harm! lying on the table. There was a white sheet over it, covering the face and all. I couldn't tell what brought it there. I nearly fell to the ground with fright. I thought at first it was somebody was killed, and the murderer had brought him to the cabin and left him there while I was asleep, to put the murder on me. How could I tell? Then I thought it was somebody was playing a trick to frighten me, being living all to myself and lonesome like. I wasn't easily made afraid then—I never cared or dreaded ghosts and all that as other people used—but this came on me so suddenly, rising out of my sleep, that I was knocked about. I was greatly knocked about. But I took courage. Anyhow, says I, I'll try if it's a joke. I came over to the table. The table used to stand up by the wall on hinges, on an iron bar, but it was now laid down flat. When I came near the feet of the table I thought I heard a voice outside the door saying, "Don't go near it, Joe! Don't go near it, Joe!"'

'I ran to the door, but there was nobody there. I ran to the gable end, there was nobody there. I ran round the house. I called out, "Who's there? For God's sake, who's there?" There was no answer. I called again ——

'"Help! Help there's somebody killed. For God's sake, come to me." There was no answer, but I thought I heard the footsteps of someone running away. I looked where the noise came from, but there was no one to see. I ran to the door again, having gone all round the house, and when I got there I shouted as loud as I could, "For God's sake, come back. I'm very lonesome. There's somebody dead, I think, and there's nobody to help me. Come back, for I'm very lonesome—come back, and God bless you." But nobody came back—nobody came back.'

The man rubbed his forehead, which was in a teem of perspiration, with his cap. His face was very haggard, and his voice was husky and broken with the terror of the remembrance. His hand trembled so visibly that the priest, listening with intent interest to his narrative, felt that a little stimulant would not be out of place, rose up, and going to a little cupboard, filled him out a tumbler of whiskey, and placed it beside him on the chimneypiece. But the man, absorbed in his painful recollection, did not notice the movement, or did not care for the drink, for he left it untouched where the priest had placed it. Still he rubbed his forehead with his cap clenched in his hand.

'Take a drop of that; it will strengthen you,' said the priest, motioning to the drink. The man extended his hand mechanically, and placed it to his lips. His hand trembled so much whilst he did it that some of the liquor spilled in the action. But he was so intent on his narrative that he scarcely noticed this, but resumed his discourse where he had left off.

'Nobody answered me, though I listened. I went inside

again. What made me, God knows, but what could I do? If I went to the barracks—'twas five miles off—what could I say?

"'A dead man in my cabin,' I'd say.

"'What happened him?' they'd say.

"'He's killed.'

"'Who killed him?'

"'I don't know.'

"'Who brought him there?'

"'I don't know.'

"'You killed him yourself.' What else could they say? If I went to a neighbour's house—the nearest was a mile off across the hill—they'd say the same thing. These things went through my mind like lightning. But there was something else—I don't know what else—urging me to go inside again. I couldn't help it, I believe. The thought of the form lying under the sheet—the knees raised up like one that was stiff and cold—had an attraction for me that I couldn't account for afterwards. So I went inside, and when I was inside the door I felt a great inclination to turn back and run off anywhere—anywhere at all from the place. But I didn't.

'The room looked dark when I came back. Maybe 'twas the light of the sun outside that was in my eyes. There was nothing to light the cabin but the door and what light came down the chimney, for the shutters were on the window. But the darkness cleared off very soon, almost as I got to the foot of the table, and It was still there. The white sheet was still over It, covering face and all. I could see where the knees had the sheet raised up. I could see where it sunk on the breast. I could see where it was raised again over the head. But what need I go on? I went to the head of the table. I don't know how I was able to do it, but I did. I lifted the sheet, and with one pull tore it away. And then I gave a cry and fell dead. I knew I gave a cry, because I heard it in my ears as I fell.' He paused again and rubbed his forehead, over which the cold drops stood like heavy dew, again with his cap.

The priest sat still looking into the glare of the burning logs in the grate, listening with rapt intentness to the strange man's story. The flickering light of the logs threw grotesque shadows of himself and the stranger on the walls of the parlour, looking bright and large as the flames lit up, and subsiding into faintness as the light declined. If the priest were given to nervous feelings there was enough in the weird story of the man, in his crouching, trembling posture before the fire, and in these giant figures, figuring on the walls, to make him feel a dread. But a long life passed in the sacred minstry, during which he had seen so much of the passions and hopes and fears of the human heart, added to a mind still strong and vigorous in its saintly and unblemished character, made him ready to shake off the illusion. So he passed his hand once more through the white hair that clustered over his temples, and patiently waited till the stranger should resume his story.

Having wiped the perspiration from his forehead, replacing his cap on his knee once more, the man continued:

'What did I see when I pulled the sheet off? Maybe a dead man, brought in while I was asleep—maybe a man that was got drowned in the torrent, and carried to my cabin as the nearest place. No. Not any of these—that wasn't what I saw. What I saw was—myself!'

'Yourself,' said the priest with, for the first time, something of a start.

'Myself. Myself, as often as I saw myself in the surface of the stream, in the looking glass, in the tub of water outside the door, or the window of a very dark night. But there was more than that.'

He paused again.

'More than that?' reiterated the priest.

'More than that,' said the stranger. 'In the single glance I took I saw more nor that. There was blood on the breast of

82

the form; there was blood on the hands, and there was blood—I saw it—on the under part of the white sheet when I turned it up. And there was a knife like that' — he produced one —whereat the priest started. As if the man noticed the start, and understood its meaning, and was sorry for what caused it, he quickly replaced the knife in his belt again. He wiped his hands in his cap as if there was blood upon them, and then applied it as before to his forehead. When he had done all this he sat silent, gazing into the fire. He sat abstracted so long that the priest deemed it necessary to quietly rouse him, to do which he stirred the logs which were beginning to smoulder. But they failed to arouse the crouching stanger.

III

There was another pause of painful silence.

'When you awoke?' said the priest.

'When I awoke,' said the man, recovering himself with a start. 'Ah, when I awoke, I think it must have been an hour after, but when I did I looked around me. There was nothing there. Nothing. The table was standing upright on the bar by the wall. There was no corpse there, and no sheet, and what's more, there was no sign of blood under the table nor on it. I staggered up into the bedroom thinking there might be something there, but there wasn't. The whole place was the very same as when I saw it in the morning when I lay down to sleep.'

'Perhaps you were asleep all the time,' said the priest eagerly catching at any explanation to remove the illusions from the tortured mind of the wretched man; 'perhaps you only dreamed it?'

The man shook his head. 'I awoke where I had fallen—beside where the table was, not in the place where I went to sleep. And besides, I remembered that in running around the house to see who had spoken, I dropped a shoe, which was only half on, heel downwards, when I went to sleep. It was off when I awoke. I went out and found it there. I slept on the heath that night, and for many nights after, and never went next or near the house.'

'And do you do it still?'

'No. I went back again after some time. The weather was getting cold, and there was a craving over me to go there—a restless craving. I don't know why. How could I?'

'After all,' said the priest, after a little reflection, 'it was probably but a dream—a waking dream. Your mind may have been disturbed—you may have been uneasy in your sleep, and you walked about. People sometimes do. In this period of walking slumber your mind may have conceived this strange impression.'

The man shook his head again as if receiving no consolation from this theory.

'It was not that,' said he, mournfully. 'I feel it was not that. I know it was not that. I don't know how I know it, but I do. But I have seen It since.'

'Ah!'

'I have seen It since. The second time,' he continued, lowering his voice almost to a whisper, and looking round as if he almost, in the quiet parlour, expected to see it again —'the second time I saw It was about the same time next year—that is, last year. I was on the mountain, as before, all the morning and, as before, I was jaded and tired searching after them where they had gone astray. I was very tired by the time I had them all gathered again in the White Lands— I notice that It always comes before me when I'm most weary and tired—and I sat myself down by the river side where the river runs very deep at the bend near ——'

'Near the trout pool,' said the priest.

'Just so,' said the man, eagerly, 'near the trout pool. The sheep were all in a crowd drinking by the river side, where the lane leads down close to the trout pool, and I sat on a stone on the bank a little way over the river. I might have been dozing. I might have been half asleep, for the morning was hot and I was tired. I was thinking of one thing or another, half dreamy like—thinking of times long ago before I came to this part of the country, and wondering how my life came to be so miserable and lonesome. Then I fell a-dozing again, and began dreaming that there was a strange dog hunting the sheep from the White Lands far over Dunmore—a black dog, I remember well.

'Just then I was woken by the rush of the sheep that had been drinking at the brink of the river. They were racing over one another in their mad haste to get away from it. I thought the dog I had been dreaming about was after them, they were making such great haste to get away. But though I looked about everywhere I could see no sign of the dog, or anything else to frighten them, and I was wondering what was driving them away pell-mell so fast. There was nothing near. The river was bright and pleasant. Just then, turning my eyes to the pool, the blood ran back to my heart—ran back so thick that I felt a weight at my heart, as if all the blood in my body had hardened there.

'Floating on the water where it was deepest in the trout pool — there It was again. There was no covering over It this time. I saw it all at a glance. I thought, too, it was partly alive. I thought It looked at me. I saw It's hand pressing over the wound in the side as if to draw out the knife that was sticking there. There was blood upon the breast, and blood upon the knife and on the water. As the eyes seemed to look at me, something awful like Death came over me, and it was God's wish I saw it no more, for I fainted on the bank.'

Once more the man paused in his narrative to wipe away the bead drops from his temples. Again the priest stirred up the half-burned logs until they blazed, and threw once more the forms of the two men in huge misshapen grotesque figures on the walls—shadowy outlines in fit keeping with

85

the strange tale to which they were listening.

'When I awoke the first thing I did as I got on my knees, for I was too weak to stand up, was to look at the trout pool. I believe I was so attracted to the spot that if I was certain of my death on the minute I couldn't help looking at it, though I was in frightful fear. But there was nothing there. On the surface of the trout pool there was nothing floating. It was calm and bright, with the summer sun on it. I thought the body might have gone down among the stones that banked up the river, and been caught amongst them, but there was no such thing. Then I remembered what I saw in the cabin—indeed, it was full in my mind all the time in a confused sort of way—and I turned to run away from the place, and the first thing I noticed as I did was that all the sheep were standing on a little hill—you remember the long mound of heath that runs along the middle of the field, next to the trout pool?'

The priest remembered it perfectly, and nodded as much, as he still listened intently, with eyes fixed on the fire.

'There, on that mound, all the sheep were standing looking down at me, or at the pool, I don't know which. Maybe they saw It as well as myself. How do I know? What else made them run away?'

He had a habit of asking questions more as a matter of form than for any answer he expected to them, or than that they required. Therefore, the priest made no answer, but listened on.

'I never went near that place again by myself. But if I met a nighbour going across the mountains or coming to look at the sheep I brought him, without telling him what for, until I brought him to the trout pool. But there was nothing ever to be seen there again. Nothing.'

There was a long pause of painful silence. The man resumed:

'Now, what does It come to me for? What does It mean?

Why does It come and go? Could nobody tell me what It means?'

The priest remained silent in reflection. The man gazed alternately at the fire and looked round the room.

'Did you see It since?' inquired the priest. He was anxious to hear the story to its conclusion before he could form an opinion, or before he would prepare to administer to the diseased mind of the man. It was a case unique within his experience. He had some difficulty in setting it down to aberration, so coherent was the man's tale, so earnest his manner of telling it. That he was suffering great mental torture, and that the torture reacted on him physically, the restless eye, the quivering, nervous movement of his hand, the bead-drops of excitement on his temples, and the thinness and emaciation of his features, not to speak of the crooked and bent form of what must have once been a powerful man, plainly showed. The priest thought that it was a case requiring great care. Fortunately, to the consolations which his religion gave, the priest was also a little versed in medicine also. He had studied it as part of the studies appertaining to his ministry in the halls of Coimbra, and a long life spent among all forms of disease, both bodily and mental, had sharpened his early studies. But this was a new type—an illustration of a mind overcome by illusions—that he had never experienced before, and he was at a loss to ascertain how far it might be actually a presentiment, and how far it might be the deceit of a wandering brain. So he contented himself, before forming an opinion, to hear the remainder of the man's story.

'Did you see It since?'
'I did. I saw It since.'
'Often?'
'Once.'
'When?'
'This day. This very day. No later. This very day.'
He paused.

87

'Ah! how did It present itself?'

Whether it was that the recentness of the apparition produced a fresh terror in his mind, or that the flow of ideas had ceased within him, a considerable time elapsed before the man shook off his torpor and conmmenced anew.

'I was out all this morning looking after the sheep again. They had gone astray again, or they had been driven astray —one or the other. I left them safe and together last night, but this morning they were scattered over the mountains. It was nearly ten o'clock this morning before they were again in the White Lands, and as I had been out since long before daybreak I was very tired when I was done. I came home to my cabin, and, as before, I lay down by the fire on some sacks of wool to sleep. I think I told you before It always came when I was tired and weary?'

'You did,' said the priest, seeing that the man this time waited for an answer.

IV

'I slept very soundly. I was dreaming—I don't know about what—but I was wakened by some one calling. I started up as the words rang through the house. At first I thought the sheep had gone astray again, and someone was calling me. I was not quite awake, but I heard someone say:

' "Get up, Joe! and go for the priest. Get up, Joe! and go for the priest. Get up! Get up!"

'I got up. I was wide awake enough now. And when I got up and looked round me, the table was laid flat again. It was stretched on the table again with the sheet over It. I felt myself getting cold all over. I felt as I suppose people feel when they are dying. And just as my eyes fell upon It, and I stood stock still with terror, I heard the words again. They came from the doorway—

' "Go to the priest, Joe; go to the priest."

'I ran to the door. I cried out —

' "I will go. Come here to me, and I will. Help me! Help me."

'I ran to the door, but there was nobody outside. I ran up into the room—there was no one there. I looked under the bed—there was no one there.

'I ran out again. I called out —

' "If there's anyone near, God bless you and come to me." I ran to the gable end—there was no one there. I ran to the back of the house—there was no one there.

'I thought I heard the footsteps of somebody running away. I couldn't see anyone.

'I shouted again:

' "For God's sake, come back! I'm very lonesome! There's someone dead I think, and there's nobody near to help me! Come back and don't run away. I'm very lonesome! Come back!" But nobody did come back—nobody.

'I waited for a bit, and then I ran round to the front of the house. And then to the doorway again. I don't know what made me, but I entered the house again. And the light was in my eyes when I entered, and the room was dark, for there was no light except what came through the door or down the chimney. The windows were shut. But while I was trying to see in the dark somebody spoke from the table—from the table—

' "Go to the priest, Joe! Go to the priest!"

' "Who's that?" said I. "Who's that— who's speaking?"

'But there was no answer. And when my eyes got accustomed to the gloom, and I began to see about me, there was nothing there. The table was standing in its place by the wall. It was gone, and everything was in the same place as when I lay down to sleep. There was neither sheet, nor candle, nor anything else. Where did It go to? What brought It there? Why did It appear to me? What am I to do?' The man paused again, and his terror appeared doubled. He shivered with terror where he sat.

'What did you do then?' inquired the priest, gravely and gently.

'I ran out. I came here. I saw you were gone out. I waited in the wood close at hand until I saw you coming back. I crept to the door, but I hadn't the courage to come in. I waited about trying to get courage to knock, but I couldn't. What could I tell? How did I know you'd believe me? How did I know but you'd say, "This man is a fool or he's mad. I'll turn him away. I'll send for the police." I daren't go away. I couldn't endure it any longer. At last I rapped. And here I am. What am I to do?' Once more he rubbed his forehead with his cap, and crouched nearer into the light and heat of the fire as if for comfort and companionship.

The priest reflected a little. His very soul was stirred with sorrow and sympathy for the distressed man. At last he appeared to have his mind made up.

'When did you go to your duty last?'

'I don't know. Not for a very long time. Not for years.'

'Do you say your prayers ever?'

'Prayers—No!'

'Not for years, either.'

'No, not for years.'

'Well, my poor friend, you must make up your mind to go at once. There will be a Station in Balmore tomorrow morning. Come to me there. You know where it is?'

The crouching man nodded his assent.

'Come to me there. Kneel down and repeat these prayers after me.'

The priest reached down a prayer book from the mantlepiece, and knelt down before the fire. The man did likewise in a crouching attitude. The priest then read a decade of the Rosary aloud—slowly, in order that the man might repeat it after him, which he did. At the conclusion he reverently blessed himself, the man following.

'Take this, and carry it with you—carry it safely.'

90

It was a small *Agnus Dei,* which he handed him. The stranger placed it with great care in his waistcoat pocket.

'Come to the Station tomorrow morning, and I promise you you shall see the apparition no more.'

'I will,' said the man, overcoming apparently some repugance he felt. 'I will.'

'Do you think you are sufficiently strong to go home, or would you prefer to stay here for the night?'

'No,' he returned. 'I'll go. I'll go look after the sheep. I feel stronger now. I'll go.'

'Well, take some of this. You want it.'

He motioned to the drink. The man took the tumbler in his hands and drank it. He prepared to go. He was at the door going when a thought struck the priest.

'That knife,' he said.

'The knife?' repeated the man, looking to where it was stuck in his belt.

'Yes. You must not wear that again. Leave it in your hut, or throw it away, or thrust it in the heath. You must not carry it again. You promise me that?'

'I will, your reverence. I'll promise you that.'

'Good night, then, and God bless you!'

The priest opened the hall door, and the man passed out into the night. The priest, standing at the opened door, watched him as he proceeded down the road, until he was lost in the darkness. His figure grew less and less distinct until he was lost completely. Then the priest closed the door, bolted it, and returned into his parlour.

He trimmed the lamp afresh, and, taking his Breviary in his hand, knelt down. He was soon immersed in fervent prayer, and continued reading prayer after prayer totally heedless of the hours that passed until he grew weary, and his sight began to fail him. Then he rose up. When he did he noticed that the first rays of the day were beginning to come in through the parlour window.

'I did not think time had passed so quickly,' he said.

Then he extinguished the lamp, and went to his bedroom, where he was soon fast asleep.

The following morning was Station morning at Balmore. The Stations were held in parts of the parish far away from the chapel, and isolated. They were chiefly intended for the accommodation of those families who could not attend the regular confession days at the chapel. They had a good effect, inasmuch as it was customary for all in the townland where the Station was held to attend at the farmer's house where it was given, and attend to their religious duties. Any one who did not was known, and immediately fell under the ban of public opinion. In this way many of those who might become lukewarm, indifferent, or heedless of their religious duties, were prevented from becoming so, and were kept in the right course.

It is, perhaps, owing to these country Stations that so truthful and genuine a spirit of religion pervades those remote districts in the country, where one would suppose, from their isolated and forgotten position, the people would soon become semi-barbarised. They had a further good effect in the fact that each farmer's house in which the Station was held got a thorough cleaning and doing up previous to the occasion, which made it clean and comfortable the whole year round.

Among those who assembled at the Station, the priest was glad to see his strange visitor of the previous night. It was the first time that he had ever attended one, although he had been two years in the place. He looked as if he were a true penitent, for, with head bowed down, not once lifting his eyes to look about him, he remained during the two hours he was waiting his turn to go to confession. It might have been abashed feeling in presence of, to him, an unusual number of people. It might have been through a desire to keep himself in a state of perfect recollection before going through a painful duty; or it might have been deep contrition for his sins. But whatever was the reason, there he was, with head bent on his breast, kneeling in an attitude of profound prayer.

V

From that time forward he was a constant attender at the Stations in his mountainy district, where they were somewhat infrequently held. But always as soon as Mass was over he took himself away. Once only did the priest afterwards ask him—it was nearly a year afterwards—at one of these Stations:

'Did the apparition ever present itself since?'

'Never, your reverence. I never even think of it.'

A year rolled by. The day on which the Station was to be held in Balmore came round again. It was held on the same day in each year, and as the priest rode along the mountainy road that led to it, he could not help remembering the stranger that had presented himself before him the previous evening twelve months ago; and that had come to confession on that day at the last Station.

In fact, for some inexplicable reason the stranger was continually running in his head during the morning, and as he looked out for him amongst the crowd of people in attendance, he failed to distinguish him. He was not there. Neither did he turn up during the Mass, nor afterwards.

It was customary after the ceremonies of the Station had been completed, for the head of the house, some intimate friend, and the priest, to breakfast together, and chat pleasantly over local affairs. In this way the latter always obtained an insight into the affairs of his parishioners, so that there was scarcely one of the permanent flock of his parish whose circumstances, habits, character, and dispositions he was not thoroughly acquainted with.

While they were seated at breakfast they were somewhat alarmed by the entrance of a messenger into the breakfast parlour to state that some strangers were below. One of the party having gone down, returned with word that they were policemen in disguise coming to arrest someone.

Seeing that this affected the well-being of some of his parishioners, the priest stood up and went to the kitchen, where they were enquiring their way.

'You are coming to arrest someone?' he said to the policeman.

'A shepherd living in this neighbourhood.'

'His name?'

'I think he goes by the name of Joe,' said one who appeared to be a sergeant.

'What do you arrest him for?' asked someone.

'Murder,' returned the sergeant. 'He has been wanted these two years or better. Murder—committed in the West of Ireland—of a cousin of his own—in a faction fight. Drove a knife into his heart. We heard he lived in this neighbourhood.'

As the priest listened to this his attention was attracted by a man riding with great haste across the field opposite the farmer's door, and never stopping or staying until he reached the door. His haste was evidenced by the fact that he rode without any saddle, and that for reins he made use, to guide his tractable animal, of a straw rope or suggawn, being the first thing evidently that had come to hand when he was starting.

He jumped off his horse breathless.

'Is Father Carty in?' he asked of some who were standing at the door.

'Yes,' said the priest stepping forward. 'I'm here—do you want me?'

'Yes, your reverence. The shepherd, Joe ——'

In his breathless haste he was unable to proceed further.

'Yes,' said the priest, while the policeman advanced towards the door. 'What of him?'

'He's dying, your reverence. You're wanted in all haste

94

at the hut. You'll hardly catch him alive. He's very bad entirely.'

'What happened to him?' enquired the priest with much anxiety, while one of the young men of the house ran to get his horse ready for him. 'What happened to him?'

'He was found dying in the trout-pool—among the stones. He fell off the cliff a little above it, following a sheep, and the stream carried him down till the stones at the trout-pool stopped him.'

'Is he very badly hurt?'

'He'll never recover, your reverence. It'll be as much as you'll do to see him alive, even if you do that much. He is very badly hurt. He had a knife in his hand, taking a thorn out of a sheep, maybe, when he fell. In the fall it went through his side. We were afraid to pull it out for fear he might bleed to death before you'd see him.'

'Where is he now?'

'He's in the hut.'

The priest got into the saddle and galloped off without more ado. The policemen took a shorter and more direct route across the hill, in company with some others whom curiosity prompted to go there. The priest arrived a little before them.

'Am I in time?' he said, as he dismounted at the door.

'No, your reverence,' replied a man standing at the door, 'you're not in time—he's dead. Dead this ten minutes.'

The priest and the police entered the cabin. The shutters were on the window. The only light there was came through the door or down the chimney. It was some time before the priest could see in the gloom, but when he did he saw a scene that had often vividly impressed itself on his imagination. The table that stood upright by the wall was laid flat, and over it there was a white sheet. Under the white sheet there was the form or the outlines of a man. The knees were raised, and the sheet was depressed over his breast, and raised again over his head.

Just as he told it.

The priest lifted the covering, looked at him, and gently laid it down again.

'You may go back, gentlemen,' said he to the policemen. 'He's dead.'

'The Lord be merciful to his soul,' said the priest, as he mounted his horse at the door. 'He suffered frightful torture in this world. If he had only kept his promise, and not worn the knife; but the will of God be done.'